FLIGHT OF THE FALCON

STAR WARS™

PIRATE'S PRICE

WRITTEN BY
LOU ANDERS

ILLUSTRATED BY
ANNIE WU

DISNEP
LUCASFILM
PRESS

LOS ANGELES · NEW YORK

Printed in the United States of America
First Edition, January 2019
1 3 5 7 9 10 8 6 4 2
FAC-020093-18334
ISBN 978-1-368-04151-5

Library of Congress Control Number on file

Reinforced binding

Designed by Leigh Zieske & Jason Wojtowicz

Visit the official *Star Wars* website at: www.starwars.com.

For Arthur

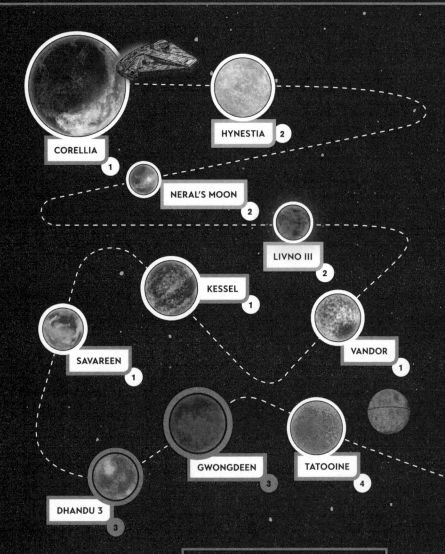

STAR WARS

CORELLIA 1

HYNESTIA 2

NERAL'S MOON 2

LIVNO III 2

KESSEL 1

SAVAREEN 1

VANDOR 1

GWONGDEEN 3

TATOOINE 4

DHANDU 3 3

FOLLOW THE ADVENTURE!

1 *Solo: A Star Wars Story*

2 *Lando's Luck*

3 *Pirate's Price*

4 *Star Wars: A New Hope*

5 *Choose Your Destiny: A Luke & Leia Adventure*

6 *Star Wars: The Empire Strikes Back*

7 *Star Wars: Return of the Jedi*

8 *Star Wars: The Force Awakens*

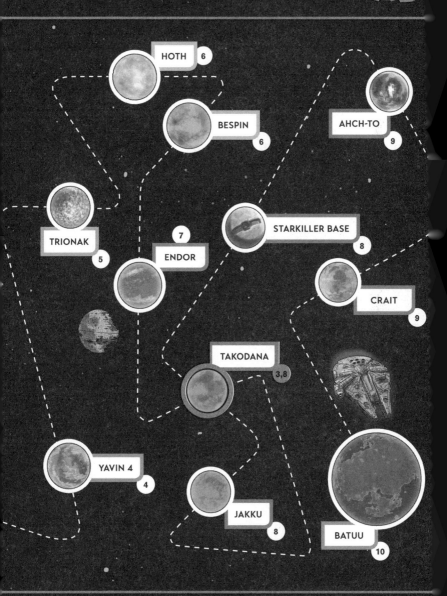

FLIGHT OF THE FALCON

HOTH 6

BESPIN 6

AHCH-TO 9

TRIONAK 5

ENDOR 7

STARKILLER BASE 8

CRAIT 9

TAKODANA 3,8

YAVIN 4 4

JAKKU 8

BATUU 10

THE IDIOT'S HAND

"Oh, the stories I could tell. So many of them true."
—*Hondo Ohnaka to Ezra Bridger*

As far as wretched hives of scum and villainy went, Bazine Netal thought that Black Spire Outpost seemed friendlier than most. Certainly, the Trandoshan running the supply company was more than willing to point her in the direction of her quarry. He didn't even ask her why she was looking for the Weequay. He just sold out his neighbor for a few credits.

She moved through the crowded streets. Although she looked striking in her black leather skull cap and Rishi eel ink–tipped fingers, no one paid her any attention. The locals were used to all manner of beings coming and going. Still, Bazine knew better than to turn her back on any of them. Especially not when she was so close to her goal.

She had been a long time getting there.

After being led on a chase across the galaxy, she had tracked the *Millennium Falcon* to the planet Batuu and its infamous port—Black Spire Outpost.

Glancing above the roofline of the buildings, Bazine could see how the place found its name. Rising above the shops and dwellings were the petrified trunks of what were once giant trees that had dominated the skies of that world. Now their blackened remains stood as silent sentinels on the outskirts of the town.

The outpost was not an easy place to find unless you knew about it first. It was located where the Unknown Regions met Wild Space, a stopover for smugglers and those of less savory occupations—a place for rogues and opportunists, con artists, thieves . . . and of course, pirates.

So it made a sort of sense that her target would be there. After all, the infamous Hondo Ohnaka had been all those things and more.

Bazine's intelligence had told her that the notorious Weequay scoundrel was there on Batuu, where he was running a shipping operation called Ohnaka Transport Solutions. Doubtless it was a thin front for a smuggling operation. But it didn't matter to Bazine what it was. She wasn't interested in his services—just his ships . . . or rather, one of them in particular.

One very special ship.

She found the old pirate in a busy cantina where a repurposed RX-series pilot droid was playing upbeat music to an audience that mostly ignored it. But there was Hondo. He was sitting at a corner table playing sabacc with a nervous-looking Ithorian, a furry Yarkora, and a grinning Suerton.

Surprisingly, the Weequay didn't even have his back to the wall. If she had gone there to kill him, he would already be dead. Fortunate for him, then, that she wasn't planning to. At least she wouldn't unless she had to. And that remained to be seen.

Still, the way he had his back to half the room struck Bazine as unnecessarily careless and ridiculously trusting. It certainly spoke to his legendary overconfidence. In fact, Hondo wasn't so much sitting in his chair as sprawling in it, a drink in one hand and three sabacc cards in the other. He wasn't playing it close to the vest, either, but swinging his sabacc cards in time with the music. As she approached him from one side, Bazine could easily glance at his hand. He had a two, a three, and the face card known as a sylop, sometimes called the idiot. He was grinning like one, too, although, judging from the pile of credit chips on the table, it looked as though the Suerton was the one who was winning the most.

"My friends," said Hondo, his voice ringing out with a happy lilt that was almost musical, "I cannot tell you how much it pains me to take all of your credits today. But you make it too easy. And as my sweet mother used to say, if you're going to bet, bet big."

He tossed an impressive handful of credit chips onto

the growing pile in the center and waited for the others to ante up.

"You're bluffing," growled the Ithorian from one of his twin mouths.

"I never bluff," Hondo replied. Then, after a slight pause, he added, "Except maybe for those occasions when I do. But this is not one of them"—another pause—"as far as you know. Which is not very far."

"So you *are* bluffing?" asked the Ithorian, confused.

"How can you be sure? I could be bluffing about bluffing," said Hondo. "Hmmm . . . or bluffing about that."

"Bah," growled the Ithorian from both mouths at once. But then the Yarkora spotted Bazine. He gave a little start, and it amused her to wonder which of his two stomachs had done a flip.

"What is it?" said Hondo. "Have I got something on my face? I mean besides my so very attractive frills?" He brushed the backs of his fingers across the barbs that grew from his jowls. They had gotten longer as he had gotten older. Perhaps he thought they made him look distinguished. But then he caught sight of the newcomer out of the corner of his eye.

"Oh, we have company, don't we?" Hondo said. He swung his legs around and turned in his chair to face her. "Well, well, won't you join us for a game . . . Bazine Netal?"

She couldn't help cocking an eyebrow at that.

"You were expecting me?" Bazine asked.

"You or someone like you," said Hondo. "I figured someone would show up eventually."

"Very well," she said. "Then you know I'm looking for—"

"Not here, not here." Hondo waved a hand dismissively. He stood, scooping up his remaining credit chips and depositing them in a pocket of his jacket.

"Hey!" objected the Suerton. "Play your hand first."

"Bah," said Hondo. "I smell bigger profits than these. Just count yourself lucky I did not take all of your money today."

Despite the Suerton's face being split in a perpetual grin, Bazine didn't think he looked happy about this.

"You were bluffing, weren't you? You would have lost the hand," he growled, but Hondo was already rising.

"I suppose we will never know, my friends."

"He was bluffing," said Bazine. "I saw his cards."

Hondo coughed in embarrassment.

"What? Nonsense. Never. But, my dear, may I suggest we move to another table, where we can talk without this riffraff overhearing?" He gestured to indicate his companions.

"Riffraff?" barked the Ithorian, and the Suerton frowned. But the Yarkora rose when they did. Bazine thought something passed between Hondo and the furry little alien, a nod perhaps. But then Hondo strode toward a table at the far side of the room, and she hurried to keep up in case he was making a run for it.

He didn't seem to be.

"You were playing with a Suerton," observed Bazine.

"So?" said Hondo. "I play with everybody who has credits to risk."

"You do know that some Suertons have the ability to subconsciously affect probability?" she asked.

Hondo stopped in his tracks.

"What? No," he said, scowling. "I thought he was just lucky. Oh, well, that explains some things. Live and learn, they say. So, can I get you a drink?" He gestured to a bizarre array of taps that lined two opposite walls of the room. Bazine noticed that the tap handles were all handmade, each one unique. Obviously, they'd been scavenged from different objects over the years, from droid arms to what she thought might be an antique lightsaber handle. But then Hondo was talking again.

"I can recommend the Fuzzy Tauntaun," he said.

"No," she said firmly.

"Are you sure? I have a wonderful relationship with the owner, Oga Garra. She puts all of my drinks on my tab. And then I tear up my tab. It's such a good arrangement. At least for me. I am not sure how she feels about it. But you can feel free to order what you like. Cost is literally no object."

Bazine frowned. "I'm here for business, not pleasure."

Hondo held a hand to his chest as though he were deeply offended by that.

"I'm shocked. Shocked at your misunderstanding," he said. "Surely, you must know that business *is* pleasure."

"If you say so."

"I do, and I am an expert on these things, but here we are."

Hondo had led her to a table in a far corner of the room. This time, the pirate did place his back to the wall, forcing Bazine to sit with hers to the crowd. The move was intended to put her at a disadvantage. It didn't. Bazine could handle herself anywhere, and she'd been in plenty of establishments rougher than this cantina. Plus, there was a certain confidence that came from wearing thermal detonators in your shoes.

She leaned across the table and stared into the goggles over the Weequay's eyes.

"I'm looking for a ship," she said.

"Oh, yes," said Hondo, smiling. "Straight and to the point. I like that about you. And Ohnaka Transport Solutions stands ready to serve you. We have plenty of ships. I'm sure we can provide any solution you might need for . . . well, for transport obviously."

"I didn't come here in need of a smuggler," she said.

"Smuggler!" Hondo waggled his fingers in the air and made a face like he had a bad taste in his mouth. "Why, the very word is an affront. No, I am merely an honest dishonest businessman making his way in a harsh galaxy the only way I know. The way my mother taught me. Not a simple sleemo smuggler scum."

"Let me clarify," said Bazine. "We both know that I'm not here for your services. I don't need anything transported, smuggled or not."

"No," said Hondo. "No, you are here for something greater. Let us stop pretending. You are here for that most amazing treasure. A real wonder in a galaxy full of wonders. You, my friend, are after the *Millennium Falcon*."

Bazine was genuinely surprised.

"How did you know?"

Hondo shrugged.

"Word gets around when one searches as much as you have done. And I am always interested in news when it carries with it the potential for profit."

"So do you have it?"

"Who wants to know? I assume you are not looking for it for yourself. You have an employer, do you not?"

"That's my business. It's not your concern."

Hondo held up a finger.

"Ut-ut-ut . . . It is my concern, insofar as this: can whoever is paying you pay me? More to the point, can they pay me a lot?"

Bazine nodded. It wasn't her credits, after all.

Hondo's smile showed all his teeth.

"Good, good," he said happily. "Then we have something to talk about. Now supposing I have the *Falcon* or I know where it is, we must talk about a fair price for such a famous ship."

Bazine started to speak, but Hondo cut her off.

"No, no. Not so hasty," he said. "You must understand, the *Millennium Falcon* is not a prize easily won—it is no ordinary ship, and if there is a chance that I will part with it, you must first understand what this means to me to say good-bye. You must know its value to me personally before I can name my asking price. To do that, you must know something of my own history with this legendary vessel. Are you sure you won't have that drink? The Fuzzy Tauntaun? Or maybe a Carbon Freeze? No? Well, then, settle back and prepare to be wowed as the great Hondo Ohnaka tells you a story. I remember it like it was many years ago. Because it was. Ah, yes, the first time that I ever saw the *Millennium Falcon*. A ship so fabulous I knew right away that I had no choice but to try to steal it for myself."

Bazine raised a painted eyebrow at this. But she settled in as Hondo had suggested. After all her travels, it looked like she was going for another ride.

PART ONE

A SHIP TO REMEMBER

CHAPTER 1

AWAKE AND CRASHING BEAUTIFULLY

The day started out like so many others.

I woke up in a strange spacecraft. I was alone in the cockpit. The control console was smoking and sparking. *Crackle, crackle, fizzle, spark!*

Oh, and it seemed that two Imperial TIE fighters were shooting at me.

Keeooo-keeooo!

It was all very exciting.

How did I get there?

I had only the vaguest memory. I recalled something about a party, excitement and dancing.

Oh, yes, and a strange drink called Sarlacc Juice. In hindsight, I don't recommend it.

Oh, and I think there was an Imperial garrison commander.

He was the one doing the dancing.

Because I asked him to.

By "asked," you understand, I mean I was firing

blaster bolts at his feet. And he was hopping about so as not to get shot in the foot. It was so amusing, for me at least. But perhaps he was not having as much fun.

Ah.

So that explained why the Imperial TIE fighters were shooting at me.

Well, there is always a price for a good time.

And this was another good time.

But all good times must end.

And the strange ship didn't look like it was going to last much longer, not with the smoking and the sparking and the shooting—*keeooo-keeooo!*—and everything coming apart around me.

So I looked for a place to land.

There was a planet up ahead.

The navicomputer said it was Galagolos V. Do you know it? It is one of those swampy, stinky planets.

Not much to look at and you have to be careful where you put your feet. But beggars cannot be choosy when their ships are on fire, I always say.

So I set down.

I went careening through the atmosphere, black smoke billowing behind me. It must have really been quite a sight.

And do you know, it was a perfect three-point landing.

By that I mean, I hit three separate points before I finally came to rest.

What was left of the ship skidded to a stop right in an empty docking bay. At least I think it was empty. There were some *bang-crash-crunch-crunch* noises at the end before I stopped moving.

I hopped out quickly. The service droids were getting excitable.

"Sir, sir, you can't dock here," they said, rushing up to me and waving their metal arms about.

I tossed them a handful of what might be credit chips. Or maybe just pieces of the control console.

"Keep the change," I said.

Then I rushed through the doors before they could stop me, and I was in the spaceport proper. I hoped to quickly lose myself in the crowd. Oh, it was a busy place for such a stinky, swampy planet. That was good. But the air was all sweaty and wet. Sticky, sticky. Nothing like the dry heat of my beloved Florrum. It was no matter. I didn't plan to stick around for long.

But to get off that stinky ball, I would need a new ship. That was, of course, merely a momentary setback for a great pirate such as myself. And there I was lucky enough to have crashed in a spaceport. Opportunities abounded for the unscrupulous and the bold. And I am both of those things.

I began to look around.

So many people. And I did not know any of them. The day was alive with possibility. I had a feeling that something was bound to happen.

And it wasn't long before something did.

You see, as I walked through the crowded streets of the Galagolos spaceport, I heard a shout of alarm. It was coming from an alleyway.

There was a young woman, human as far as I could tell. What did she look like? Like any human. She was about so tall. With hair.

I saw that she was being menaced by two nasty-nosed Cloddograns.

"Go away and leave me alone," she said, and though she might have been afraid, her voice was strong and determined. Of course, that was none of my concern. It is a rough galaxy after all, and we all must learn to take care of ourselves. Which is what my sweet mother said before she threw me out the first time.

So away I walked.

But as I continued on, I noticed the unwelcome presence of stormtroopers. The bucketheads were moving around the spaceport. They seemed to be asking questions, talking to the locals. And I, Hondo, was getting funny looks—and fingers pointing in my general direction. Were the stormtroopers looking for me? Well, I did arrive in a ship shot down by TIE fighters. It was just possible that the two things might be somehow related.

I needed some way to appear less conspicuous. The bucketheads were probably looking for a lone Weequay who matched my description. Well, I could not change my looks. But perhaps I could do something about that "lone" part.

An idea occurred to me.

So I turned and headed back to the alley where I had seen the woman. She was still struggling with the Cloddograns. In fact, a fight had broken out. I had to admire the way she was holding her own, even when it was two against one. And when fighting Cloddograns, the odds are even worse than usual, because they have twice as many arms!

"Hold it right there, you ruffians!" I yelled, reaching for my blaster.

There was only one problem with that.

I did not seem to have my blaster anymore. I must have lost it in the Imperial garrison.

It's these little details that will get you into trouble, my friend, every time.

"Who the kriff are you?" growled one of the Cloddograns as I stood pointing my empty fingers at him.

"Who am I?" I said. "Why, it is me, Hondo Ohnaka!"

"Never heard of you."

Now, I admit I was stunned by that.

"Never heard of Hondo Ohnaka, the famous pirate? My exploits are legendary." When that received only a blank stare, I continued. "Why, I once had a crew that was feared throughout the galaxy. I was notorious, famous, infamous. I have captured a Sith. I have fought with and against Jedi. I was a friend to Jango Fett and Obi-Wan Kenobi both. Why, my bulbous-nosed friends, you have never met anyone as interesting as I."

The two Cloddograns just glanced at each other and shrugged.

I turned to the young woman. But she gave me an apologetic look, as well.

"Sorry," she said.

"Not ringing a bell?" I asked. "Not even a tiny one? Jingle, jingle, jingle?"

Nothing. Just blank stares. It was too much.

"The galaxy has such a short memory." I sighed.

Then I reached out and grabbed each of the Cloddograns by their sticky bulbous noses, and I smashed their heads together. *Smash, smash!*

"Run!" I shouted at the woman as the Cloddograns fell to the ground.

And then we were running, the young woman and her daring rescuer.

"Down!" she yelled, shoving me aside.

Twin blaster bolts flew over my head. *Bdew-bdew,* they went. I saw the blast marks sprout on the wall like little black flowers of death, appearing centimeters from where I had been. So it seemed that she was saving me.

And then we were running again, Hondo Ohnaka and his daring rescuer.

Well, wasn't that an interesting day?

Fortunately, we were both fleet of foot. We soon outdistanced the Cloddograns. When there was no sign of our pursuers, it seemed safe to stop running. We paused in a narrow alleyway strewn with refuse from a filthy diner, and we leaned against a wall slick with swampy humidity to catch our breaths.

"Thank you for stepping in," she said.

"For stepping in what?" I asked, checking my boot. You can never be sure on Galagolos. But then I realized she was thanking me for helping her, the noble way I had put myself forward.

"You are welcome," I said. "But you were doing quite well yourself. You must have some training in the martial arts. It is hard to fight a species with so many arms. Thankfully, they do not have so many legs, or we might not be as fortunate to have outrun them." She gave a little laugh, and I asked, "But why were they bothering you?"

Something haunted passed across her face then, but she shook her head and said, "Probably they just wanted credits."

"Credits," I said, my ears pricking up. "Do you have credits?"

The suspicion in her eyes wounded me, so I let it go.

"I am sorry. I was just making conversation. Permit me to introduce myself. I am Hondo Ohnaka."

"The famous pirate," she finished for me.

"So you have heard of me after all?" I said, brightening.

"No," she said, taking the wind out of my solar sails. "I'm just repeating what you said."

"What I said, yes." I sighed.

As we talked, we began to walk, heading back toward the docking bays.

"Forgive me for asking," she said, "but why would a pirate come to my assistance? Isn't that a little noble for a buccaneer?"

"But a pirate *is* noble," I replied. "At least when he wants to be. Have you not heard of a pirate's honor? It is a wonderful thing. Like the honor of thieves. And anyway, Hondo has always had a soft spot for the underdog."

As we moved through the streets of the spaceport, I saw the stormtroopers again, and I got nervous. But my hunch was correct. The bucketheads walked right past me without giving me a moment's thought. They were looking for a desperate fugitive, not a dashing man walking and talking with a young woman like they were old friends. My deception had worked!

We got to the docking bay, and I remembered I was there for a new ship. It was time to part company.

I turned to take my leave of the woman, but she was looking at me searchingly with her deep intelligent eyes.

"But you *are* a pirate, aren't you?" she asked. "And

you knew how to handle the Cloddograns. So maybe you can help me with something else. I'm looking for a specific ship. It's very important that I find it quickly. If you could accompany me . . . I might have a need for someone like you."

"Have need of me?" I said. "Hondo is not a lackey. Were you not listening? I once ran the famous Ohnaka Gang. I am not just some piece of hired muscle."

"I thought you had a soft spot for underdogs," she said.

"It is not *that* soft," I said. "I am very sorry, my dear, but one rescue is enough, and I have my own problems. I have engaged in quite enough heroics for today."

"What about your pirate's honor?" she said.

I snorted. "That is the wonderful thing about a pirate's honor. Conveniently, it turns on and off as needed. Turn on, turn off. Turn on, turn off. This morning I am honorable. This afternoon I am a scoundrel. And I think I am ready to be a scoundrel again."

And then I left her there, looking surprised and maybe a little stung. And I went off on my own once more.

Did I feel bad about it? Perhaps. But I confess I was still grouchy that no one there had heard of me. Me—the leader of the once-feared Ohnaka Gang. Me—the pirate who once held Count Dooku, Obi-Wan Kenobi, and Anakin Skywalker hostage all at the same time! And stayed friends with two of them! In fact, I

once kidnapped Ahsoka Tano and her six Jedi younglings, and then I rescued Ahsoka Tano and her six Jedi
younglings from another kidnapping all in the same
week. Come to think of it, for a notorious pirate, I sure
helped the good guys out of tough times on many occasions. And I only caused one or two of those occasions
myself. I even fought in the Liberation of Lothal. Now
that I mention it, I'm still waiting on payment for some
of my services. Plus, I'm the only one in the galaxy who
ever found the lost treasure of Kanata's castle. All that,
and the young lady didn't know who I was! How could
the galaxy forget so much?

Now, this may come as a surprise, because I am always
such an upbeat guy, jolly Hondo, but being alone on a
strange planet and not being recognized made me feel
something.

It had been some time since I parted ways with my
fellow Weequay. I had lost my pirate empire. I had lost
my wonderful base on Florrum. I had even lost dear
Pikk Mukmuk, my Kowakian monkey-lizard. Let me
tell you, you never truly appreciate a monkey-lizard
until it is gone. And I should know. I've lost a few.

So I was adrift. I had been going it alone, by myself,
making my way as a small-time pirate where once I was
the scourge of the galaxy. Oh, how far the mighty had
fallen! There was a hole in my heart that needed to be
filled. And it would not be filled by being that young
woman's goon. No, I needed a ship, the kind of ship I

could use to get a new crew. Then I would be back on top! Then I would make the galaxy remember me again!

So I went to the docking bays, and I began to look for the perfect vessel to fly me away from that swampy, stinky planet.

The first ship I found was too small. The next ship was too big. I needed a ship that was just right.

And there, in the third bay, was the most magnificent ship ever!

But it was heavily guarded, so I went to the fourth bay.

And there she was.

At a glance, she looked like any other YT-1300 Corellian freighter. Not too special right? But then I saw there was something different about her. She had been altered in several ways, and I had a pirate's hunch—a feeling, if you will—that there was more under the access panels that was not showing.

You know the ship I mean? It is not hard to guess. Of course, at the time I did not yet know its name, but it was the *Millennium Falcon*. And I must say, my old heart began to go pitter-pat, pitter-pat, pitter-pat. And I felt the hole in my soul—the big, gaping hole. I knew then it was a ship-sized hole. Because with the right vessel, a person can do anything. And if that person happens to be Hondo Ohnaka, why then he can do anything else, too! And that—that was the right vessel.

Well, there was only one thing to do in response to

such sublime grandeur. I, Hondo Ohnaka, would have to steal the ship for myself.

The boarding ramp was, of course, closed. But I am somewhat more experienced than most in the matter of, ahem, shall we say *liberating* starships from their former owners. And so I know little tricks you may not be aware of. For instance, few people know that there is a small access hatch adjacent to the boarding ramp on the YT-1300 light freighter. And I was going to make use of it.

The Hondo Ohnaka Method of Starship Liberation involves some wiggle and some waggle.

First the wiggle. I reached into my pocket, and I pulled out a small but very valuable pouch. With such a pouch, a pirate can make himself welcome anywhere. You see, it contained a selection of key bypasses of various sizes. And a key bypass is a very useful tool. I selected a long one. This I slipped into the seam of the access hatch—and with a wiggle of my fingers—I quickly used it to slice through the lock.

Then it was time for the waggle.

Making sure I was unobserved, I hoisted myself into the hatch. It was tight going, but I didn't have to go very far in—just far enough that I could reach the ship's computer systems. Then from the pouch I took another device—a data spike. Most people would use the data spike to try to override the ship's defenses. Sure, if you want to do it the most pedestrian way. But I am Hondo

Ohnaka. I did not try to override the ship's systems. No, I tried to make the ship *like* me. So I put all the great things about Hondo Ohnaka into the ship's memory, and I told it how much fun it would be to let me in. That was the waggle. And to my satisfaction, I heard the pop of compressed air releasing and the welcome *vvvvmmp* noise of the boarding ramp lowering for me.

And so soon I was in the cockpit. Right away, I began to input the prelaunch sequences. My fingers itched to take the control wheel.

But despite bypassing the security and sweet-talking the computer, I found the controls were temperamental, the programming of the ship's computer unorthodox. It was almost as if the ship was still reluctant to let me take her. Still, some of the modifications were most impressive. It was just going to take some getting used to on both our parts. But I suspected it would pay off, and fortunately, I would have all the time in the galaxy. Or so I thought.

I heard the babble-babble of voices. They were coming up the boarding ramp. That was most unfortunate. The previous owners of the ship had returned before I had finished stealing it.

I realized then that I should have raised the ramp first thing.

It's these little details that will get you into trouble, every time.

"Think fast, Hondo," I told myself. I did one more

thing to the ship's controls, a kind of insurance policy for later, and then I looked around for a place to hide.

"*Arrrrgooooroooo!*"

Something very large and very irritated was making a growling, groaning noise.

"Well, I don't like the smell of this muck ball any more than you do, Chewie," someone else answered. "But we'll be leaving just as soon as our passenger gets settled."

And then I heard their footsteps going to the cockpit.

I wondered what a Chewie was. It sounded like something to eat. But alas, I could not wait around to find out. I needed off that ship, and fast. So I started to emerge from my hiding spot and make my exit, but then I heard a third person coming up the corridor. Obviously, it was the passenger who had hired the ship.

And then—oh, no—there was the *vvvvvmp-vvvvvmp* of the boarding ramp rising, and the *zzzzvoooooom* of the ship's engines powering up.

We were taking off. I had no way out without being seen.

I was trapped.

And just like that, I, Hondo Ohnaka, went from being a famous pirate to a mere stowaway.

Well, wherever we were going in that magnificent modified freighter, I hoped it was someplace interesting.

CHAPTER 2

OUT OF THE FOOD UNIT, INTO THE TRASH COMPACTOR

Well, we were off in no time, zipping through space going who knew where. What an adventure it was. But so far, I did not see a way to make a profit. In fact, if I wasn't careful, there was a good chance I might find myself tossed out an airlock. And that, my friend, was not an experience I was keen to have.

I mentioned that the ship had been modified quite extensively. Fortunately for me, one of the many changes was that she was riddled with hidden compartments. Doubtless they were meant for smuggling contraband, but now I was smuggling myself in them. Never let it be said that I don't appreciate irony!

And please do not insult me by asking how I, Hondo Ohnaka, greatest pirate in the galaxy, was able to find these compartments if they were hidden. Come now, there is not a trick in the book I have not tried myself. I know a hidden compartment when I see one. Or rather, when I don't see one, if you catch my meaning.

So I stayed quiet, and hidden, and I used my ears to find out what I could. And I peeked through the tiny cracks in my hidden spot. For a bit I didn't see anything or hear very much, just the routine conversations coming from the cockpit. "Velocity indicator" this and "acceleration compensator" that. "What's that warning light doing, Chewie?" *"Grrrarrrbrrrr."* That sort of thing. Blah, blah, blah.

But once the course was laid in and the ship was on its merry way, its pilots began to move around. It seemed there were only two of them, plus their passenger. Perhaps if I needed to, and I had the element of surprise, I might be able to overpower them and take control of the vessel for myself. It is good to keep your options open.

"All right, lady," said a man. "We've cleared the atmosphere. So now, how about you tell us what's so important about the third moon of Dhandu that you're willing to pay ten thousand just to leave right away?"

Ten thousand for a ride. That was a grossly inflated price for a relatively short trip. Whoever the pilot was, he was ripping off his passenger. I admired him instantly.

Also, now I knew that we were going to the third moon of Dhandu, and very rapidly. That was interesting. As my sweet mother once told me, "Hondo, someone else's urgency is your opportunity." Perhaps I could find a way to profit yet from that day.

So I settled in to listen carefully.

"Dhandu's third moon is just the first stop," said someone else. The voice was that of a young woman. And it was very familiar. I began to suspect that I had heard it before, just a little while before. Destiny sometimes throws the strangest things our way, does she not?

"What do you mean 'first stop'?" asked the man. And he didn't seem too happy about it. But then, he had not seemed happy about anything since I first heard him board the ship. He was kind of a grumpy guy. "Now look here, lady, you only paid me enough for one flight."

Actually, she had paid enough for three. Oh, how I admired him.

"I don't have any more credits," the woman said, and I felt my interest in the conversation dipping. "But if you listen to what I have to say, I can promise you a whole lot more than just ten thousand."

Suddenly, my interest was back. And growing.

"I don't know about this," said the man. "I don't like jobs that change the terms after we're underway."

"If you'll just hear me out," said the woman. "To begin with, my name is Mahjo Reeloo. And my business, let's just say I'm a fellow scoundrel like yourselves."

"What makes you think we're scoundrels?"

"Mostly the reputations you've been spreading yourselves," said Mahjo.

"*Hrrruh, hrrruh, hrrruh.*" Laughter from the Chewie.

"Yeah, yeah, yuck it up," the man replied. Then to the woman he said, "Go on."

"Well, the truth is that I'm after a huge score."

"How huge?" said the man. Straight and to the point. A scoundrel after my own heart.

"Huge," Mahjo said. "Bigger than huge. A collection of Novian rubies being kept in a safety-deposit box in a shielded vault on Gwongdeen."

Now that was interesting. Novian rubies. They are very rare, very valuable. In fact, no one had seen any Novian rubies in over thirty years. The pirate who could steal them would have quite a prize indeed.

But the man wasn't having it.

"Well, that's it, we're out," he said in his gruff voice.

"No, wait," began the woman.

"Lady," he interrupted, "everyone knows the Undervaults of Gwongdeen are impregnable. You can't break in there. It's impossible. I knew whatever you were going to say was too good to be true."

"They're impregnable, yes," said Mahjo. "But they're easy to get into if you have a key."

There was a pause, during which I could almost hear wheels turning in the man's mind.

"And you have the key?" he asked.

"That's why we're going to the third moon of Dhandu," Mahjo explained. "Because the owner of the safety-deposit box is on the moon right now."

"Well, isn't that great. I suppose he's going to just give it to you?"

"Well, no," said Mahjo. "I thought we'd steal it from him."

"'We,' huh?" said the man. "Sorry, lady, you hired me to be your pilot, not your thief or smuggler. I'll take you as far as the moon, but then you're getting off."

"I assumed you'd jump at the chance," she said. "Isn't this the sort of thing you do all the time?"

"I like jobs where I get paid up front. And passengers who are straight with me. Picking heists that have no hope of being pulled off isn't my idea of a good time."

"But I have to get inside that deposit box! I have to! Please."

Well, the woman sounded pretty desperate. She must have wanted those rubies for something very important. And where there is great desperation, there is also great opportunity.

So I took that moment to reveal myself.

Emerging from my hiding place, I cried, "Hello! Friends, this is your lucky day. You need a pirate for the job! My name is Hondo Ohnaka, and I just happen to be such a pirate!"

Well, you can imagine I made quite an entrance.

Three jaws dropped at once. The woman's, the man's, and the big, furry brown creature's—which I now recognized. Suddenly, all the growls and grunts made sense. It was a Wookiee.

Unfortunately, I found myself looking at the business end of a blaster and a bowcaster.

"Who the blazes are you?" the man said. He was young, with brown hair, wearing a cropped brown jacket, knee-high boots, and a thigh holster. His outfit had a kind of slapdash swashbuckling look to it that I appreciated, the connoisseur of fashion that I am.

"Did you not listen? I am Hondo Ohnaka, here to solve your problems. But just whose blaster barrel do I have the pleasure of staring down?"

"The name's Solo. Han Solo. And this is Chewbacca. But wait . . . I'm the one asking the questions here, mister. How did you get on my ship? I don't take kindly to stowaways."

"A stowaway!" I said. "Why, the very word is distasteful in my mouth, even if it is circumstantially true. But I am no *mere* stowaway. I am a pirate, a great pirate. And today I am the answer to your prayers."

"I didn't pray any," said Solo. Then his eyes widened in sudden realization. "A pirate, eh? You weren't stowing away. I bet you were trying to steal my ship when we came back!"

"See?" I said. "You've only just met me, and already I am demonstrating the very credentials you are looking for!"

Well, the man made a face at that—the kind of face that says, *Let's just shoot him now and toss him out the airlock later.* I thought it better to move the conversation forward. So I glanced around. "This is a very unusual freighter. May I know the name of this fine vessel?"

"You haven't heard of her?" said Solo, looking a little bit crestfallen. "This is the *Millennium Falcon*."

"The *Millennium Falcon*! What a coincidence!" I cried. "My last ship was called the *Centennial Peregrine*."

"No, it wasn't," he objected.

"Why not?" I said. "You can't prove it wasn't. Anyway, I stole it and crashed it in the same day. After that, it is a small thing to name it, too. Or do you want it to have died without a name?"

"I'm sure whoever you stole it from had their own name for it."

"You raise a good point, my friend. With such clever insights, I can see this is going to be a very profitable partnership."

"This isn't going to be anything." He turned to the Wookiee. "Chewie, toss our pirate here out an airlock."

A furry hand grabbed me by the collar.

Now, if a Wookiee wants to toss you out an airlock, out an airlock you go. Possibly in several pieces. So I turned to the woman, this Mahjo Reeloo. She was looking at me, overcome I assume with joy at seeing me again—but also, it must be admitted, with some confusion.

"My dear friend, it is good to see you again so soon. Before I am unceremoniously and so rudely excluded from your expedition, will you please tell this fine Wookiee that you asked me for my help earlier this very day?"

"I did ask for his help," Mahjo said to Chewbacca. "After he helped me against some angry Cloddograns. But . . . you didn't know I was here. You couldn't have . . . you couldn't have planned to steal the very ship I was chartering."

"I didn't need to know. That's how good I am. Things just have a way of working out when Hondo is involved."

At that moment, a voice came over the ship's comm.

"Attention, unidentified Corellian freighter, you are believed to be harboring a suspect wanted in conjunction with an incident at Imperial Garrison Bardelberan 7."

"What?" said Solo. "I'm not harboring any suspect." He looked at Mahjo Reeloo.

"I've never been to Bardelberan 7 in my life," she said.

"Never?" he asked.

"I don't get around much," she replied.

Then he looked at me.

"It's you, isn't it? What did you do to get them so riled up?"

I gave him my most endearing smile.

"Whatever it was, I'm sure it was a misunderstanding. But there is no sense crying once the bantha milk is spilt. Perhaps now would be a good time for you to demonstrate just how fast the *Millennium Falcon* is."

"Or maybe I just hand you over to them." Then Solo turned and ran to the cockpit. We all followed him, where we saw, making its approach toward us, a TIE/sh shuttle. With that ship, the Empire could cut its way in if we did not open an airlock.

But I had no fear. I knew Han Solo was bluffing. After all, he was the pilot of a ship with many, many compartments for smuggling contraband. Obviously, he was a man who wanted to keep his secrets. I doubted very much that he wanted the Empire boarding the *Falcon* any more than I did.

"Am I the only thing on this ship for the Empire to find?" I asked. And again I flashed him my so endearing smile. "Is there nothing else you want to keep out of their hands?"

Surprisingly, it was Mahjo Reeloo who answered first.

"They can't search us," she said. "Really, they can't." She sounded so very insistent. I wondered what she was carrying—and where she was carrying it.

Solo looked from me to the woman and back. Then he turned to look at his big fuzzy friend. The Wookiee shrugged his enormous shoulders.

"Perfect! This is just perfect!" Han Solo paused and pointed his finger at me in a most annoying fashion. "Whatever happens, I'm holding you responsible for all of this."

Solo activated his comm unit.

"Negative on that boarding. We have, uh, an escaped swarm of, um, Sortuvian brain moths currently infesting our cargo hold. You wouldn't want to board us."

"Corellian freighter, that is not acceptable. Please stand by and prepare to be boarded."

"Um, I don't recommend it," stalled Solo. "The brain moths haven't been fed in several rotations. They, um, look pretty hungry. For, um, brains."

"That is not our concern," said the voice on the comm. "Our boarding party will be wearing their helmets. They're rated against Sortuvian brain moth bites. Now comply with our instructions or we will open fire."

"No, um, these have, uh, very big teeth."

Solo gave us an apologetic look.

"*Mmmmmmmrrrrrr,*" complained Chewbacca.

"You want to give it a try?" he asked the Wookiee.

"Do you think maybe they bought it?" asked Mahjo.

And then came that delightful *keeooo-keeooo* sound as our pursuers fired warning shots.

"Does that sound like they bought it to you?" said Solo. "We're under attack."

CHAPTER 3

HAN SOLO FLIPS OUT

Keeooo–keeooo went the laser cannons.

They were still warning shots, but soon they would be the real thing.

Solo was powering up the hyperdrive as fast as he could and began to input the coordinates for Dhandu.

Meanwhile, I looked out the window and saw that the TIE shuttle was very close.

"My friends," I said, "now would be a good time."

Solo grumbled at that, but then he grinned. "I suggest you both hang on. You wanted to see what the *Millennium Falcon* can do? Baby, show them what you can do."

He flipped a switch.

And the ship made a noise—a kind of powering down sound. It went *dvvv—vvvvv—vvvvvv—dnkkk.* . . .

And nothing happened.

"That is . . . um, most impressive," I said, trying my best to be positive in what must have been an embarrassing situation for him.

"What?" Solo hollered. "Chewie! Where's my hyper-drive?"

He began to frantically flip switches. He even banged a fist on the console. Then he turned a face to me that was almost comical it was so angry.

"You messed with my ship! Didn't you?"

Keeooo-keeooo went the laser cannons.

K-toom! K-toom!

No more warning shots. The *Falcon* rocked under the blasts from the TIE's cannons.

"I resent your implication," I said as I regained my balance. "And here I thought we were starting to be friends."

K-toom! K-toom!

Solo frantically flipped a few more levers.

"We're not friends," he said. "Now what did you do?"

"Not friends?" I was wounded. "Companions at least? Would you say we are friendly acquaintances?"

"No!" shouted Solo. "We aren't anything! Now tell me what you did."

Keeooo-keeooo! More laser cannons.

K-toom! K-toom! More rocking of the ship.

"What. Did. You. Do?"

"Now that I think of it," I said, "I might have placed an interrupt on the conduit to the hyperdrive or something."

"An interrupt!"

"Or something."

"To my ship?"

"In my defense, I thought you might be angry discovering me on your ship, and I might need some insurance."

"That doesn't make me like you any better."

"But it does make you need me now," I said.

Keeooo-keeooo! K-toom! K-toom!

"Will you two stop arguing," said Mahjo, "and fix it!"

I started to reach for the controls, but then I hesitated.

"Not until he says that Hondo is coming with you. You all agree that I am a part of this big heist on the Undervaults of Gwongdeen? We are equal partners in this endeavor?"

Keeooo-keeooo! K-toom! K-toom!

I put on my best sabacc face.

"Or we can all sit here and wait to be boarded. If we are not blown apart first."

Solo looked like he would prefer to shoot me. But he growled, "I'll consider it."

"Well, that I can work with."

"Good. Now fix my ship."

I scooted him out of my way—"Scoot, scoot, scoot"—and set about removing the interrupt on the conduit to the hyperdrive.

"See? Already Hondo is helping the team."

"We're not a team," said Solo.

"Grrrrrrrraaaaaarrrrrph," said Chewbacca.

"You know I don't like people touching my stuff," said Solo, and he shoved me rudely aside. But the hyperdrive powered up correctly under his hands. It made a pleasant humming sound.

"Grrrgaaggaa," said Chewbacca.

"Don't thank him," said Solo. "It's his fault it was broken in the first place."

Keeooo-keeooo! K-toom! K-toom!

We were shaken fiercely on our feet as the TIE shuttle fired at us at what was nearly close range.

"Now is not the time to argue over who broke what," I said. "You were going to show us what the *Falcon* can do."

"Hang on," said Solo. "This time for real."

"Aarrr wgh ggwaaah," said Chewbacca.

And then we heard the wonderful *fffffffvooooom* as the *Millennium Falcon* jumped into hyperspace.

We had made it!

"Oh, that gets the heart pumping," I said as we all gazed at the welcome kaleidoscope of blue lights swirling before us. "I find last-minute escapes are always the best, don't you agree?"

Solo gave me another of his exaggerated stares.

"We wouldn't have had to make a last-minute escape if you hadn't sneaked aboard my ship in the first place."

"True, true," I said. "Fate has indeed brought us together."

"That's not what I meant," said Solo. "Chewie, we can still toss this joker out the airlock if we want."

"*Awwwrrrrrrrr,*" said Chewbacca with a nod. That was neither agreeing nor disagreeing, so I thought it best to move the conversation to better topics.

"Tell us your plan, Mahjo. Tell Hondo, how are we going to get our Novian rubies, eh? You know they are quite rare and valuable. Enough to make every one of us very rich."

At the word *rich,* I saw Solo's eyes screw up and go all far away. Greed is a wonderful thing, especially if it stops a Wookiee from tossing you out an airlock.

"You really think you can get in the Undervaults?" he asked. And I knew that we were heading for profits.

"I can," she said. "If he can get our key."

"And I can get your key," I said. "Acquiring things is a specialty of mine."

So Mahjo Reeloo told us of her plan.

Now, this is the daring bit.

Have you ever been to Gwongdeen? Have you seen its vast Undervaults? You must have heard their reputation for security. People come from all over the galaxy to put things there they do not want other people to have. Or in some cases, to leave things for other people to come and pick up—messages that cannot be intercepted. It is a very secure place for anything that needs to be kept safe.

You see, the safety-deposit boxes of the Undervaults

of Gwongdeen are very special. Each owner is given a unique key, and the key has a special code. As long as the owner is carrying it, the code resets once every standard rotation. But if the key is lost or stolen, well, the code will not reset the next day, and the key will no longer work. And there will be no way to open the box. Very clever. Very secure.

Now, the owner of the box with the rubies, he almost never visited Gwongdeen. But he was right then on the third moon of Dhandu. And Dhandu was just on the very outer edge of what a fast, fast ship could fly in a day and still hope to reach Gwongdeen before the key code expired and time was up.

"So that's why you needed the *Falcon*," said Solo.

"That's right," said Mahjo. "She's the only ship that can get me from Dhandu to Gwongdeen in time to use the key. That is, if she's as fast as you say she is."

"She's fast, all right," said Solo.

"*Arrrrggggg,*" said Chewbacca.

"Good point, Chewie. We can get you there, but how do you lift the key without its owner knowing it's been taken?"

"That, my friends, is where Hondo comes in. If I am part of your venture and promised a fair and equal share of the profits."

"I don't know you, and I don't trust you," said Solo.

"You said you would think about it," I reminded him.

"I'm still thinking," said Solo. "And I don't like it any better."

"I vote we let him in," said Mahjo. "He helped me before, and I believe he can do what he says he can."

"Thank you, my dear," I said to her. Then I turned to the Wookiee.

And I surprised everyone once again when I said, *"Grroooogrrraaaaawrrrrrrrrrmph."*

You may not know it, but Hondo can speak Shyriiwook, the language of the Wookiees. I am good with guttural tongues, though I confess I speak Ugnaught with a slight accent. I "oink" when I should "groink." But what I said then to Chewbacca was an old Wookiee proverb. It is hard to express in Basic, but it goes something like this: "People often mistakenly judge a tree by its branches, but a wise Wookiee knows its strength is in its roots."

Well, that surprised Chewbacca. He looked at me differently after that. Perhaps he realized there was more to old Hondo than he'd at first thought. Then he turned to Han Solo and shrugged.

"Fine," said Solo, "side with him if you want to. I don't care. I just hope we don't all come to regret this."

"Then it's settled," I said, slapping my hands together with enthusiasm. "So on to Dhandu we go, and to profits!"

"There better be profits," said Solo. "Now get out of my cockpit."

I clucked my tongue at his rudeness, but Chewbacca offered to show us to the main hold, where we would be more comfortable anyway, and where he had a holochess table we could play to pass the time.

"Thank you for your hospitality, my friend," I said to the Wookiee. Chewbacca shrugged. "You are nicer than some."

"*Grrrrraaaarrrrr,*" said Chewbacca. It is hard to translate, but essentially he was apologizing for his companion's behavior. Wookiees are actually very polite, in their Wookiee way. You have to be polite when a misunderstanding can easily result in someone getting their arms pulled from their sockets.

"There is no need to apologize," I continued. "I see there is a depth of friendship between the two of you, one which will only grow."

"*Mmmmmmmrrrrr,*" agreed Chewbacca.

"You misunderstand," I said. "If I may give you some advice, I would warn you against such attachments, which can only lead to heartache, or the destruction of your base on Florrum."

You see, I had a strange feeling—a kind of hole in my chest that I thought could only be filled with the *Millennium Falcon*, or perhaps some Novian rubies.

Chewbacca responded with another Wookiee proverb. It was about a type of native tree that joins roots with others underground. I knew what he was doing.

He was implying that my status as a loner was a weakness. But, alas, that was a truth I was not yet ready to hear.

So I thanked him, and I sat down for a game of holochess with Mahjo.

She, of course, could not understand anything Chewbacca said.

"What was all that about?" she asked.

"He was just looking forward to our enormous profits," I lied as I sent my Ghhhk to attack her Grimtaash.

"You know," said Mahjo, "there is more to life than profits."

"Oh, that is a good one," I said, nearly busting my side with laughter. But then I noticed she wasn't smiling.

"Oh," I said, "you were being serious."

"I just mean, sometimes you have to do things for a higher reason."

I studied her then.

"My dear, there is the Empire. And there are those who live under the boot of the Empire's rules. Then there are those few brave souls, like myself, who make their own rules."

"And no other path?" she said. "Nothing that would make a difference for those under the boot?"

"What an interesting thing for a fellow 'scoundrel' to say. You are certainly unique, Mahjo Reeloo."

"No, I'm not," she said sharply.

"I did not mean to strike a nerve," I said.

"I'm not unique," she said, a hard edge to her voice. "I'm not unique at all."

Well, it was strange how quickly the atmosphere in the room had become uncomfortable, so I tactfully changed the topic of conversation.

"Tell me again," I said, "how did you find out about this box full of rubies?"

"Let's finish the job first," she replied. "Then you'll have your answers."

I might have objected, but then she sent her Savrip against my Monnok, and I had to concentrate on the game.

After a little while, Chewbacca returned to tell us we were arriving. We crowded into the cockpit as the *Falcon* came out of hyperspace—*whoomp!*—and the stars slammed into place around us. And there, through the transparisteel viewport of the cockpit, we saw the third moon of Dhandu in front of us. It was a pretty little yellow-orange satellite hanging in space—like a fruit inviting us to take a bite. And I must say, Han Solo and Chewbacca were quite the seamless team as they navigated the *Millennium Falcon* flawlessly from the cold vacuum of space into the atmosphere of that small and pleasant-looking world. They were like brothers, if one brother were covered in fur and the other were a grouch, and I wondered what had transpired between them, the man and the Wookiee, to make them two halves of a whole. And again I felt that gap in my soul, only I wondered if it was ship-shaped after all.

But then we were below the clouds. We saw great, rolling auburn-colored grasslands that stretched from yellow sea to yellow sea. And as we descended, a huge sprawling city came into view ahead of us. But immediately we noticed there was something different about it.

The city seemed to be undulating just like the grasslands, rocking and swaying and . . .

"Are my old eyes playing tricks on me?" I said. "Do I need to clean my goggles or is that city moving?"

"*Grrrrrrrrgaahga,*" said Chewbacca, agreeing with me.

"You took the words out of my mouth," I replied to the Wookiee.

"What kind of place are you bringing us to, lady?" asked Solo.

"I don't know," said Mahjo Reeloo. "I've never been here before. I just know the key we need is here now."

So we all looked, and we saw that the city was indeed moving across the grasslands. And what was more, bits of the city weren't staying put even within itself. They seemed to be shifting around, churning and reorganizing, as though the different districts were jockeying for position.

"Wait a minute," said Solo. "This isn't a city at all. It's a creature. This place is alive!"

Well, as we made our approach, we saw that Solo was both right and wrong.

You see, as we would soon learn, Dhandu 3 is home to a colossal species. There is a type of reptile, very, very big. The locals call it a turlossus. And the turlossus has a large shell on its back that is flat on top, like a vast plateau. And it walks around all day on its six enormous stumpy feet, sucking up the grass of the grasslands in front with a cluster of great proboscises and, well, you don't want to know what it does in back but you can guess. Grass goes in, grass goes out. And those giant creatures move about in herds, great numbers of them all walking and eating together and doing their business across the moon forever—never stopping, not even to sleep.

Now, you wouldn't want to build on that moon, because you might get stepped on. The turlossus are not aggressive, but neither are they particularly careful where they place their feet. So even by accident, it would not matter. There you would be, asleep in your house, or maybe taking a shower, or watching a holovid and—*squish-squash!*—flat as a bantha-butter pancake you would be. You can see how this would spoil a pirate's day.

But the inhabitants of that moon of Dhandu, they have to live somewhere. So they have found a clever solution. They have built their cities on the backs of these giant creatures. Whole neighborhoods and districts can fit on one of the larger animals. And as the turlossus walk around together in their herds of twenty or so creatures, so their cities are always strolling around the moon. It is truly wonderful! You can go sightseeing without even leaving home! Can you imagine? Every day a new horizon. Perhaps I will retire there one day—if I can find an old pirates' home.

Now, it is a fact that these gentle giants are slow enough in their movements that clusters of them can provide the surface for villages and towns, though on occasion someone's house or establishment might wander off and join another herd. Catwalks and bridges are raised and lowered between locales, but of course, no one place stays in its position relative to any others for long. So finding your neighbor or your favorite eating hole from day to day can be a bit of a challenge. You might leave your house to go to work in the morning, only to find it isn't where you left it when you come back at night. Such a situation would make life interesting, wouldn't it?

At any rate, shortly we set down at a spaceport that had been constructed near the tail end of one of the larger creatures. We prepared to disembark. And that was when we got our second surprise.

"Wait, wait!" clucked the flightless, feathered inhabitants of the moon. They were rushing up to us as we stepped onto the boarding ramp, holding out pairs of clunky ankle bracelets that they wanted to put on our feet.

"You need these if you're going to walk," said one of the Dhanduese.

"Buddy, I can walk just fine without any strange device on my legs," said Solo, and he took a step off of the loading ramp.

And then, like magic, he sprang into the air.

"Chewieeeeeee!" he shouted.

And we all watched as Han Solo went sailing away across the docking port, flipping over and over and over, like a bird himself. Like an ungainly, awkward, and very angry bird.

CHAPTER 4

A PIRATE, A SCOUNDREL, AND TWO SMUGGLERS WALK INTO A BAR

Solo was flying through the sky.

"Look at you!" I cried. "Bounding through the air like a Jedi!"

I was trying to be positive. Unfortunately, he did not land so much like a Jedi. Their landings are somewhat more dignified and probably far less painful. As I winced in sympathy, one of the locals rushed over to assist Solo.

"We tried to warn him," another said.

"Believe me, you cannot tell that man anything," I said. "But what exactly has happened to him?"

"This is an extremely low-gravity world," the local explained. "All visitors to the moon are required to wear special gravity weights strapped to their ankles to keep them grounded."

"That makes sense," I said. "Obviously, it would be very bad for the tourists otherwise. If they all went flying off into the sky, how could they spend their credits? Step, step, bye-bye!"

I turned to my remaining companions.

"We must put these on our ankles if we are to walk here."

Well, Chewbacca, he had a hard time with this. I believe he thought that the bracelets looked too much like manacles. And I wondered what had happened to the big guy to make him so skittish. Clearly, he did not like anything that reminded him of being fettered. But after he tried to pull a foot away and ended up doing an unintentional backflip in the low gravity, well, I said something to him in Shyriiwook comparing his feet to the roots of brave trees, and he let the little feathered people attach the weights to his legs.

Now, the Dhanduese themselves did not wear these ankle bracelets. Their clawlike feet were prehensile, and they used them to grip the ground. It worked for them, but I felt it was slightly sad—these wingless birds holding on tight so they would not fly.

As the bracelets were slipped around my own ankles, I noticed that the locals had little blinky-blinky sticks. The sticks had readout displays and buttons to adjust our ankle bracelets, making them heavier or lighter as needed. I tucked that information away, in case it was useful later. You never know what you might need, but as my sweet mother taught me, a smart pirate is always prepared for any eventuality.

And so we were off again, Mahjo Reeloo leading us

across catwalks and bridges as we made our way from neighborhood to neighborhood, from one turlossus to the next. While Solo was grumpy after his impromptu flight, I was enjoying myself thoroughly. Sometimes it is important to stop and smell the blueblossoms, they say. And as we went, I tried to learn what I could about my companions.

"You seem to have a lot of information," I said to Mahjo. "What is in the safety-deposit box. Who has the key. Where they will be. Where to find Han Solo and Chewbacca."

"I've just been plotting this job for a while. And Solo and Chewie aren't hard to find if you visit the space-ports and ask around."

"People talk about their exploits?"

"They talk a lot about themselves. And they seem to get in a lot of trouble. But it is—very important—that we succeed."

"Because you want the Novian rubies? That I under-stand. They are rare and wondrous. But there are other ways to make money. Is there more to it?"

She gave me a funny look then.

"It's not just the money."

"Not just the money. Ha, ha, that is another good one."

"Don't you ever want to make a difference in the gal-axy?" she asked.

"A difference? Of course I do. I want to make a difference in my credit amount. I want it to go up and up and up."

"For once I agree with you, pirate," said Han Solo. I didn't like the way he put a sour note on the last word though.

"You say 'pirate' like it is a bad thing," I said to him. "A pirate is a noble professional. He meets his enemies face to face. If not always in a fair fight, at least he gives them a chance. Not like a mere *smuggler*, who hides like a roach-rat, scuttling about in the dark."

"Watch who you're calling a roach-rat," said Solo. "I can change my mind and have Chewie toss you off this turlossus as easily as out an airlock."

We were at that point crossing a bridge that swayed in the winds. I looked down between the planks under my feet at the grasslands far below.

"Perhaps we are getting off on the wrong foot," I said.

Solo gave me a funny look. Perhaps he thought I was making a joke about his disastrous first step off of the *Falcon*.

"Relax, my friend," I said. "In some ways, you remind me of myself as a young man."

Solo snorted at that, but Chewbacca gave me a questioning *"Arrrgrrr?"*

"You?" I said. "You remind me of a carpet I once owned."

"Grrrrrupmprrr!" Chewie growled.

"Now, now," I replied hastily, "no need to take offense, my hairy friend. It was a very nice carpet."

I don't know that it was the best thing to say, but I meant it sincerely.

Finally, we got where we were going.

"There he is," said Mahjo.

She pointed to a pavilion over our heads, where many people were gathered enjoying drinks and the view over the grasslands.

I saw a young man, human, tall and skinny with wild, frizzy blue hair sticking out the very top of his head.

"Look at him. He reminds me of an electrostaff I used to wield," I said. "Who is he?"

"His name is Jayyar Lu-wehs," explained Mahjo. "He's no one. Just the spoiled son of a weapons merchant, who comes here to wine and dine his boredom away."

"I feel better about robbing him already," I said.

"I didn't think you felt bad about it before," said Solo, giving me a funny look.

"I never do. But now I feel even better."

"So how do we get the key away from him?" Solo asked.

"Have a little faith in old Hondo," I said.

"I don't have faith in anything," he replied. "Except myself, and maybe Chewie. So I need to know before you go running in there with some half-baked plan," said Solo.

"Well, my friend, it is all a matter of deflection and suggestion."

I stepped into an empty alleyway, motioning for my companions to follow.

"You see, unless you have the twelve eyes of a Vuvrian, most people can only focus on one thing at a time. So the way to take something off a mark is to tell them you are going to take something else."

"Ridiculous," said Solo.

"No?" I replied. "I'm going to take your belt buckle."

"Over my dead body you will," said Solo, bristling.

"No, no, nothing so extreme. But I am going to steal the buckle nonetheless. Say, that is a mighty fine jacket you have there." And at that I stepped in and began to finger the fabric of Han Solo's jacket. "And where did you get this shirt?"

I moved my right hand across his chest and shoulders, touching and talking, my eyes never leaving his. It irritated him, I could tell, but half his attention was on the hand that was doing the poking and prodding while the other half was protecting the belt buckle, because that was what he thought I was after. He kept slapping my fingers away, and I kept smiling and moving them.

Then with my left hand, I held up something else.

"Look here. Is this your blaster?" I asked.

"Hey!" shouted Solo. "Give that back."

"*Hrrrr hrrrr hrrrr,*" laughed Chewie in his Wookiee way.

"But how did you do that?" asked Mahjo. "Weren't you going after his belt buckle?"

"No, the blaster was my target all along," I said. "But by giving Solo something else to worry about, and distracting him more with my slightly-too-familiar compliments about his tailoring, and my poking and prodding, he could not notice when I eased his blaster out, and tah-dah—it's mine."

"Not anymore," said Solo, reaching out to take his gun back. "And you won't be taking that again."

"Not unless I need to." I smiled. "But you see? It works. Leave it to Hondo, and we will have our key in no time."

So we crossed a swaying platform to the next turlossus, and we made our way up a flight of stairs to the pavilion. And there was Jayyar, laughing and joking with his hoity-toity friends. Behind him was a Gigoran, nearly as big as Chewbacca but with cream-colored hair. The Gigoran did not seem to be enjoying himself. He was not drinking or eating but was eyeing the crowd warily with yellow eyes. I thought he might be a servant, perhaps a bodyguard of some kind. That would be a little more complicated. But I was optimistic.

I pointed at a passing service droid with a tray on its head.

"Somebody buy me a drink," I said.

"Buy your own drink," said Solo.

"I am short on credits at the moment," I explained. "And anyway, I need it for a prop."

Grumbling, Solo took a drink off the droid. Then he took a sip of it first before handing it to me.

"Keep your smuggler germs to yourself," I said.

"Relax, Hondo, I thought you only needed it for a prop," he said with a cocky grin.

Well, I grumbled a bit at that but not for long. Hondo is never down for long—not when there is profit in the air.

So I walked into the pavilion, swinging my step like I was just another rich patron enjoying the wonderful day.

"Jayyar Lu-wehs!" I called out. "As I live and breathe. How have you been?"

Jayyar looked up at me then, a puzzled expression on his skinny face.

"I'm sorry—do I know you?"

"Do you know me? Ha, ha, what a kidder. Why, Jayyar, I have known you since you were a youngling only so high." At that I held my hand out like so, and then I glanced over the pavilion rail down to the ground far, far below. "And now look at you! You are even higher!"

It was a little joke, but Jayyar did not smile.

"Are you sure you belong here?" he asked. He frowned as he took in my clothing, which I admit was a little rough for the establishment. I may have a flair for fashion, but it is a pirate's fashion, after all.

"Is this person bothering you?" the Gigoran asked. The hostility he felt toward me was evident even through his translating vocoder.

"Bothering? No. It is I, Honda Ohnaka, friend of Jayyar's father and not a pirate up to no good. But my, what a nice timepiece you are wearing! Would you give it to me?"

"Give it to you?"

"I do not have one, but I think I loaned one to your father just like that. Perhaps it is the same one."

And then, of course, I directed all Jayyar's attention to his timepiece. He was still confused by my clever deception and wary I might be trying to steal something from him or otherwise trick him in some way.

But as I ran my free hand through his various pockets, I was not finding any keys to any safety-deposit boxes. That was very confusing to me, because I knew from Mahjo the key must always be somewhere on his person or very nearby or it would cease to function. But it wasn't on him. Not at all.

"Look, I'm sorry, but I really have no idea who you are," said Jayyar, stepping back and pushing me away. "I don't want to be rude, but I'm going to rejoin my companions now. If you like, I can have Sluncan here buy you another drink."

"Sluncan?" I said. We were both looking at the hairy Gigoran. "You don't buy your own drinks?"

"No, my bodyguard keeps all my valuables," said Jayyar. "It's safer that way, don't you think?"

"And . . . you trust him with your things? What if he wanders off?"

"He's never more than a meter from my side."

Always within a meter. Well, that was bad. It seemed the key wasn't on Jayyar Lu-wehs' person at all. It was on his hairy companion's. And that was more difficult. Because the Gigoran did not have any pockets. Or if he did, I could not see inside all that hair.

"I see," I said. "Well, I am sorry you do not remember me, Jayyar. Perhaps another time then."

I stepped back so I was alongside my companions.

"Han Solo," I said, "the key is not on Jayyar. It is on his fuzzy bodyguard. We need a new plan."

"What do you have in mind?" asked Solo.

"I'm going to compare you to something unsavory, say dianoga droppings, and you are going to throw a punch at me."

"You call me that, you better believe I will."

"No, I mean, I need a bigger distraction if I am to get the key."

"A distraction, eh?" said Solo. "I think we can arrange that."

"Okay then, here I go," and I shouted loudly, calling Han Solo a festering pile of dianoga droppings.

"What did you call me?" he roared, really playing it up for the crowd.

"You heard me," I said. "And don't get me started on this overgrown Ewok you keep around."

Then Solo threw a punch, and it went—*crack*—right on my chin.

"Hey," I whispered, "remember this is acting."

"Gotta make it look good," said Solo with a grin. "Anyway, this is the first time I've enjoyed myself all day."

So I gave him a shove, and he shoved me into the Wookiee, and the Wookiee tossed me at a table, and I got up and shoved Solo into another table. Maybe I shoved a little too hard, because he collapsed the entire table and sent a plate of glowblue noodles and chav flying over a group of Pakiphantos. Do you know the Pakiphantos? Well, it seems that they are not a good species to anger. And these, I could tell, were angry, because their big ears all flapped out wide on the sides of their heads, like big angry fans. And they rose from the table, knocking it over, and they lifted their trunks in the air and trumpeted loudly.

And one of them hauled Solo to his feet and sent him flying back into me. And like that, I was crashing into the Gigoran, which was just what I wanted to do. Although I maybe didn't expect to get so many bruises doing it.

But in the jumble and the tumble, I slipped my hand

into the thick fur and out it came with a safety-deposit box key! Yes, Hondo is that good!

Unfortunately, though, there was then quite a fight on the pavilion that we had started. But if we could slip away, I was sure things could get better.

Then one of the Pakiphantos suddenly said, "Hey, it's Han Solo."

And then another shouted, "Han Solo! You double-crossing no-good son of a bantha."

Well, so much for things getting better. I supposed they were about to go the other way.

CHAPTER 5

JUMPING JEDI

The fighting stopped.

Solo looked hard at the Pakiphantos who had just spoken.

"Trunc Adurmush? Is that you?" said Solo.

"You know these gentlemen?" I asked. "Obviously, I am using the term 'gentlemen' loosely, but do you know them?"

"Surprised to see us, aren't you, Solo?" said the one called Trunc. "Well, isn't this our luck? You can pay for the lunch your friend spilled, and the fifteen thousand credits you owe us."

"Fifteen thousand? It wasn't more than eight," protested Solo.

"You borrowed eight," said Trunc. "But you stole another seven."

Solo spread his hands in a soothing gesture.

"Guys, listen, whatever it is, I'm sure it's a misunderstanding."

"Oh, there's no misunderstanding," said Trunc Adurmush. "We Pakiphantos never forget."

"I'm a little short on funds right now," said Solo.

"That's too bad," said Trunc, "because we never let go of a grudge, either. So I guess we're going to take this out of your hide."

He raised a flat stumpy appendage that ended in four large round toenails on a pillar-like foot. Personally, I thought he could do with a pedicure.

"Now we're going to show you one of our favorite traditions. You'll love it, Solo. It's called a stomp."

"Stomp! Stomp! Stomp!" called the other Pakiphantos.

Solo gave us a sheepish look.

"It was four thousand credits at most," he muttered.

"Well, gentlemen," I said to the Pakiphantos, "this has all been very entertaining, but I can see you have business, so Hondo will say good-bye and leave you to it. And may I wish you all a happy stomping!"

"Not so fast, buster," said Trunc. "If you're with him, you stay."

"He's no friend of mine," said Solo.

"I am wounded by that," I said. "Although, under the circumstances, I also appreciate it very much." I turned to the one called Trunc. "So you see, you don't need to go to the extra effort on my account."

Trunc shrugged.

"We like stomping. And you did spill my lunch."

So things were about to be unpleasant. And there wasn't much to be done about it.

But then one of the local Dhanduese birdfolk came running up.

"No brawling on the pavilion!" he squawked. "You are all under arrest."

He held up a blinking-blinking stick thing and hit a button.

And suddenly, it was like someone had fastened huge weights to my legs.

"I can't move my feet!" cried Mahjo.

"*Grrrrrwwwwwrrr,*" Chewbacca pointed out wisely.

"No!" yelled Trunc. "I want to stomp! I want to stomp!"

"Excuse me, my friend," I said, waving for the attention of the bird person. "On what charges are you arresting us?"

"Disturbing the peace. Inciting violence in a public establishment—"

"Say, that is a very nice timepiece you have," I said.

"What? Leave my timepiece alone. . . ."

And as his beady eyes followed my one hand, with the other—I removed his blinky-blinky stick.

"Oh, I like this," I said, holding it up to look at the buttons.

"Give that back!" squawked the Dhanduese.

"Hondo," said Solo warily, "what are you doing?"

"You might say I am pondering the gravity of the situation," I said. "And now, my friends, fly! Be free!"

And I shut off all the gravity weights on everyone's feet. Suddenly, things felt very light.

"Jump, my friends, jump!"

Chewbacca roared, and Solo, who had already crashed once that day, looked most uncertain.

But Mahjo understood.

"Back to the ship!" she yelled. Then she leapt, and we watched as she went flying into the air.

Well, I had the key, and if I had the ship, too, there was no need to wait around, was there?

So jump I did, as well.

It was something, let me tell you. I was flying through the air, waving my arms and wondering where I would stop.

I soared right off the turlossus and into another neighborhood entirely. Fortunately, I have some experience with being hurled through the sky (but that is another story), so I was at least a little prepared. I landed on a street one creature over.

Ahead of me, there was Mahjo.

I glanced behind me, and I saw that Chewbacca and Solo were doing the same.

Indeed, they soon landed beside me.

But we were not free, because Trunc and the other Pakiphantos, their gravity compensators were shut off, as well. And then they were bounding through the sky, trumpeting loudly through their trunks in what I thought was most likely and rather unfortunately a battle cry.

"*Bawruuuuuuhuuuraaaa!*" they trumpeted.

And then we were off, bouncing up and down. But where were we going?

"Hey," Solo said, "does anybody remember where we parked?"

I looked and understood. The turlossus had all moved about, and the docking platform was not where we left it. Where was our ship?

Unfortunately, we did not have long to ponder, because then a blaster bolt went whizzing by—*bdew*—and then another—*bdow*. Oh, things were heating up.

Chewbacca aimed his bowcaster.

"No, my friend!" I shouted. "That is a bad idea."

But the Wookiee was not to be discouraged.

Chew! Chew! it went.

And Chewbacca went hurtling backward.

"*Grrrrrrrrrraaggoooorrrrrrrrr!*" he shouted as he zipped away.

The recoil was too strong, you see. In the low gravity, it sent the Wookiee flying.

Unfortunately, Chewbacca missed the city platforms and fell between two turlossus. We saw him drop away to the grasslands far below.

"Chewie!" shouted Solo. "I'm coming, big guy." And he bounded after his hairy companion.

"Well, there goes our ride," I called to Mahjo Reeloo. "But don't worry, you and I can pilot the *Millennium Falcon* ourselves."

She shot me a look as charged as a blaster bolt.

"How can you think about abandoning them?" she said.

"I can think about many things. Every day is full of possibilities."

"And stealing their ship?"

"More like borrowing it for an indefinite period of time," I replied.

"You're unconscionable," she said.

"I'm a pirate," I replied. "It comes with the territory!"

"Well, I'm going after them even if you aren't." Then she leapt away. But the scorn in her voice, the disappointment—it wounded me, I tell you. I didn't want to leave things like that.

Okay, she was also the only one who knew which safety-deposit box the key fit.

"Oh, well," I said. "I suppose today is another day for heroics!" And I turned on my pirate's honor and threw myself after my companions.

Bdew—bdow!

The Pakiphantos were hot on our heels. That was impressive, because I don't think their feet even had heels. Or ankles for that matter.

But there they were, jumping after us, their ears

flapping in the wind and their trunks trumpeting. *"Bawruuuuuuhuuuraaaa! Bawruuuuuuhuuuraaaa!"*

Well, the grassland was soft where I landed. I looked and saw my companions. We were all bounding on the ground. And that presented its own problems. The great, plodding legs of the turlossus were ever a danger.

"Aaaaaiyeeeeeeeee!" screamed a Pakiphantos as a foot crashed down on him from above. And then, yes, he was a bantha-butter pancake.

Solo was leaping wildly, firing his blaster behind him. And the Wookiee, too. I started to yell for him to stop, but then I watched in amazement as Chewbacca did a sort of somersault in the air, twirling over and shooting his bowcaster behind him so when the recoil shoved him, he went in the direction he wanted.

Wookiees never cease to amaze me!

One of the Pakiphantos was hit. He fell to the ground, and then—*CRUNCH!*—another pancake.

Giant feet were swinging everywhere. We were leaping and dodging between them. And blaster bolts were racing over our heads.

Bdow-bdew!   *Chew-chow!*   *Bawruuuuuuhuuuraaaa! Bawruuuuuuhuuuraaaa!*

It was crazy. It was dangerous.

It was quite a thrill!

"Look at us!" I cried in my excitement. "We are like jumping Jedi! Oh, the Force is with us today."

"The Force isn't with anyone," said Solo, "least of all an old Weequay pirate con man."

"Well, no matter," I answered him. "Hondo is a force all to himself!"

Now, you will recall I had lost my blaster, but I did a very fancy jump off the legs of a turlossus, and I went careening into a Pakiphantos, and he went spinning out of control and—*CRASH-CRASH*—he knocked himself out on the hard hide of the giant creature. Maybe he would be okay in the grass, if he did not get stepped on. Though I would not envy him being left behind the herd. You will recall I talked about what came out the other end!

Too late. *Splat-splat!* Oh, it was a bad day to be that Pakiphantos.

But then Trunc Adurmush was ahead of us. And he had his blaster out. He was lining up a shot.

"You're going to pay one way or another, Solo," said Trunc. "I told you we Pakiphantos never forget. We can hold a grudge for years."

"Yeah, that's the problem with too much looking back," said Solo, and he pointed. "You don't pay enough attention to what's ahead of you."

"I'm not falling for that," said Trunc.

"Falling? No," said Solo, "quite the opposite."

"What?" said Trunc, beginning to look around despite himself.

One of the giant, questing proboscises of the turlossus came snuffling up behind Trunc.

Slurp, slurp, slurp!

Suddenly, the Pakiphantos was sucked into the air.

With a scream of "I won't forget this!" he disappeared up the giant snout.

And then with a cough, a sputter, and a sneeze, the animal shot him out in a glob of nasty yellow-green stuff, and we saw him sail away through the sky.

Well, after that, we leapt more carefully, and we made our way in great bounds back to the top of the creatures. And there she was, the *Millennium Falcon*, waiting for us.

"My friends," I said, dialing the gravity compensators of the blinky-blinky stick so we could all walk again, "things are looking up!"

But they were also looking down. Because although Trunc had gone bye-bye, his gang was still there. And as we raced up the boarding ramp of the *Millennium Falcon*, we saw them heading to a trio of small single-pilot fliers.

"A hasty exit is called for," I said to Solo as he and Chewbacca ran to the cockpit.

"For once I agree with you, old man," the smuggler called back.

"Old? I am not old!" I said. "Distinguished perhaps. Seasoned, like a fine chuba stew."

"Reeloo," called Solo. "Shut him up and you two get into the gun wells now!"

"Come on," Mahjo said, grabbing my arm. "Fun's not over. There's shooting to do."

"Well, that is a good suggestion, I must admit."

So we were off to the gun turrets, Mahjo going up and I going down. And then I was sitting in the swiveling chair with my own laser cannon. I must say it felt good, but it made me nostalgic. I used to have a wonderful WLO-5 speeder tank. Oh, that beauty could pack a wallop, let me tell you.

But no matter. I was behind a laser cannon as Solo and Chewbacca were lifting off.

Unfortunately, Trunc Adurmush's gang was also lifting off.

I saw the three sleek little fliers now. They were Z-95 Headhunters—very durable multipurpose starfighters. I approved of the choice immensely. What I didn't approve of was that, unfortunately, they were shooting at us.

Ba-boom!

"Hey!" I yelled. "That ba-boom was louder than it was supposed to be. I really felt that!"

"I don't believe it," shouted Solo from the cockpit. "The rear deflector shields are offline! This is perfect, just perfect!"

"I don't think 'perfect' is quite the right word, my friend!" I yelled back.

"Look out!" said Mahjo, who had noticed something on the Headhunters. "They've modded their ships with proton cannons!"

"Well, you've got to admire someone who thinks big like that," I said. "Solo, can the *Falcon* take a hit from a proton cannon with the shield down?"

"We've still got capital-class hull armor," Solo responded. "She'll hold for a while."

"How long is 'a while'?" I asked.

"We don't have 'a while,'" said Mahjo. "Every minute we spend here is a minute closer to the key code being useless."

"Priorities, lady!" Solo yelled. "That key won't do you much good if we're blown to bits trying to leave this moon."

"What do you propose to do about it?" I asked.

"This," said Solo.

And with that he sent the *Falcon* into a dive.

"What?" I yelled. "Who taught you to navigate? Space is that way! Up, up, not down!"

"I know where space is," Solo said. "Look, even with our hull enhancements, I don't want to give these guys a clear shot at our backsides with our pants down when we clear the atmosphere. So you two concentrate on picking those fliers off while I concentrate on not getting hit."

And there we were, weaving in and out of the legs of

the turlossus, the Pakiphantos in their Z-95s shooting at us, lasers flying past, *whzzz-whzzzz*.

It was a good thing my gun turret was facing backward, because I think I would have been dizzy if I were watching where we were going.

Then a proton torpedo was whizzing at me.

A blast from Mahjo's laser cannon, and it blew up harmlessly in the air.

Then I fired my cannon. *Bbu-bbbu-bbbu-dew!*

With the last shot, I struck the wing of a flier. Unbalanced, it spun out of control to explode against the giant leg of a turlossus. The skin of the creature wasn't even bruised. Sadly, I cannot say the same for the pilot.

"I got one! I got one!"

"Great. You can give yourself a medal later," said Solo. "Right now, worry about the other two."

"Right," I said. "The other two."

But then Solo flipped the *Falcon*, up and over, nearly scraping the underside of the creature.

For a moment, we had shaken our pursuers.

Then one of the little fliers appeared and zipped behind us. I was staring right into the face of a grinning Pakiphantos.

His proton cannon was lining up for a shot.

At such close range, perhaps the *Falcon* could take it. But Hondo Ohnaka could not. Was that to be the end?

"*Grrrrafffffffffffgrrr!*" shouted Chewbacca.

Katooom! went the laser cannon.

My heart was in my mouth.

Ba—ba-boom!

The explosion billowed out, spreading all around me like a fiery web but not touching the ship.

I checked myself.

"I am alive! I am alive!" I said.

Yes, my friend, thanks to the mechanical genius of the Wookiee, the rear deflector shield was back on just in the nick of time.

And then Solo was racing upward, from atmosphere to vacuum, and I had never been so glad to see space as I was in that moment.

The hyperdrive engaged, and I waved a happy bye-bye to the last of the Pakiphantos.

And away we went.

I joined Mahjo in the main hold.

"Well, that was a bit of excitement, wasn't it?" I said. "But surely, now, it will all be smooth sailing from here on out."

Fafoom!

The *Falcon* suddenly rocked violently, shaking us all.

I was thrown off the bench and knocked to the floor.

"What in space was that?" I shouted.

CHAPTER 6

A BUMPY RIDE LEADS TO A BAD TURN

"**H**ave those fools fallen asleep at the controls?" I asked Mahjo as she gallantly helped me to my feet. "I tell you, Hondo should be flying this ship."

"Let's go see what's happening," she suggested. "I'm sure it's nothing." But when we arrived at the cockpit, we found Solo and Chewbacca in a most agitated state.

"What's going on?" Mahjo asked.

"Something's interfering with the hyperspace lane," Solo replied. "I'm reading numerous mass shadows."

"Mass shadows?" Mahjo gave me a questioning look. I realized she did not know what they were. We cannot all be pilots, after all, but a self-professed scoundrel used to traveling the backwaters of the galaxy should have encountered them before. I filed my suspicions away for later.

"Supermassive objects in realspace such as suns, enormous planets, things like that," I explained. "They distort hyperspace. The gravity of these large objects

creates these 'mass shadows,' which can be very dangerous. So our navicomputer plots courses to avoid them."
I turned to Solo. "So why are these here? Have you
plotted the coordinates wrong?"

"I plotted them fine," said Solo.

"You were in a hurry," I pointed out.

"I'm always in a hurry," he snapped. "Listen, old
man, the *Falcon* has one of the most advanced navicom-
puters in the galaxy. She picked the right hyperspace
lane, believe me."

Beside him, Chewbacca nodded.

"Really?" I asked. "How did two such scoundrels as
yourselves get such a fabulous navicomputer?"

"That's a story for another time," Solo replied.

"Very well. But if this is the right hyperspace lane,
then what is causing these shadows?"

Solo gave me an exasperated look and opened his
mouth to say something.

Then the ship rocked again. All of a sudden, a most
disconcerting sight met my goggled eyes. The familiar
blue kaleidoscopic tunnel of hyperspace vanished as we
were thrown savagely back into realspace. But strewn
across the velvety blackness, there was a fury of flowing,
spirally burning matter.

And we were heading for a very big chunk of it.

"Look out!" cried Mahjo.

And someone screamed. Okay, perhaps it was me.

Solo gritted his teeth as he twisted the grips on the control wheel inward.

The ship rose in a steep climb.

And we missed being smashed to death by mere meters.

But we had only avoided the immediate danger. Smaller bits of the burning space gunk thunked against the *Falcon*'s shields. *Thunk-thunk-thunk.*

"*Grrrumpg grrrumpgh grrrrrgeeeer,*" said Chewbacca, consulting the navicomputer to see what was going on.

"Of all the luck," moaned Solo. Then he explained what Chewbacca had said for Mahjo's benefit. "It looks like the main star of the Throffdon system went supernova twelve hours ago," he said. "That's just two and a half parsecs from the midpoint of this hyperspace lane."

"Of course," I said. "The supernova would have ejected its material in at least a ten-parsec radius. That is what threw us out of hyperspace. There are going to be a lot of bumpy rides in this region today."

"Just a bumpy ride?" asked Mahjo.

"My dear," I said, "when I said 'bumpy,' what I meant was, any starship fool enough to be navigating this course today may find itself smashed into a million tiny pieces and scattered across light-years."

"So what do we do?" she asked.

"The smart thing," said Solo, "would be to get clear of this debris and wait for the navicomputer to plot us an alternate route. Of course, then the trip will take longer. Maybe days longer."

"We can't!" said Mahjo. Again, I was struck by the intensity of her insistence. "If we don't make it in a standard rotation," she continued, "we might as well not go. And we can't not go. Do you understand me? We can't not go!"

"Lady," replied Solo, "I said that was the *smart* thing. I didn't say it was the only thing."

"Do you mean . . . ?" I asked.

"Strap in, everyone," said Solo. "We're going for the bumpiest ride of your life."

And with that, he pushed the control throttle of the *Falcon* forward, and we sped ahead into nearly certain doom.

"We just have to get through this," Solo explained, "and then we can get back into the quickest hyperspace lane."

"Getting through it is the impossible part," I said. "Well, it's been a good life for Hondo. I just hope you all can say the same. Because this is foolishness even for fools."

My words, let me tell you, were not exaggeration. The space ahead was thick with the burning remains of the Throffdon star. And Solo and Chewbacca piloted the ship back and forth, between and around it all, swerving this way and that, that way and this.

It was nerve-racking. It was fraught with the possibility of instant death.

And the exploded star stuff, it wasn't sitting still like good little blazing boulders of death for us to steer around. No, it was all moving—spinning over and over and twirling around at phenomenal speed.

"Look out!" I said as a large fireball sped toward us.

Solo spun the yoke to the left and worked the foot pedals in tandem, and the *Falcon* banked, veering away in the nick of time. Although we avoided a collision, we were not free. We heard a horrendous thunk as the aft shields of the ship were impacted.

"That was very close," I said.

"I'd like to see any other pilot manage it," said Solo with a cocky smile.

"I wasn't complimenting you," I explained. "A few meters less, and we would all have been smashed apart."

"You don't shut your mouth," said Solo, "and you may find yourself smashed apart anyway. The Wookiee way."

I glanced at Chewbacca, who shrugged. But then Mahjo Reeloo hollered.

"Look out!" she said, pointing. Two more masses of burning stellar matter were heading at us from opposite directions.

Solo rolled the *Falcon*, tumbling over and over so the fiery masses passed under and above us, nearly touching.

It was most disconcerting.

But then we were clear, at least of those two immediate threats.

"You know," I said, "perhaps the Novian rubies are not worth this risk. If we returned to Dhandu, we could kidnap and ransom Jayyar. If his father is a weapon merchant as you say, he could probably pay us nearly the same value of the rubies."

"No," said Mahjo. Perhaps a little too insistently. She saw my reaction, and she added, "I mean, the rubies are worth a lot more than any ransom."

"I'd pay any ransom right now if I could get you two to shut up," said Solo as he rolled the ship again to avoid a large burning blob coming directly at us. "Or does the idea of being smeared all over space appeal to you?"

"Technically," I explained, "I think if we get hit, we would be pulverized, not smeared."

Solo muttered something rude under his breath.

"I was just trying to be helpful," I muttered back. "There is no need to be snippy."

Then we were dipping low and flying high to jump two more burning chunks of dead star. And I marveled at how the *Falcon* could perform such maneuvers—well, marveled and also felt a little queasy. Fortunately, we Weequay have strong stomachs. It would be embarrassing to vomit all over the cockpit at a time like that. Still, I considered finding my way to the ship's bathroom, but no. If was about to die, I wanted to see it coming.

Or maybe I did not.

Because ahead of us, the exploded stellar matter was spread in a band so thick that it blotted out the stars. It was like a wall that filled our viewscreen, so much burning matter was there, with only the barest glimpse of space beyond.

"Well," I said, "there is no getting through that. You have done well, but we have to stop."

"No, wait," said Solo. "There's a gap."

I looked where he pointed, and I saw a small opening in the flow of fiery death. But it was closing rapidly as five different masses of blazing star stuff all converged to seal it off.

"Solo," I said, "you have done well. But not even the fastest ship in the galaxy can get through what lies ahead of us before it closes. You must stop."

"*Grrrrrrrumph,*" agreed Chewbacca.

"I'm not giving up," said Solo.

"Mahjo," I asked, "are your Novian rubies worth dying for? Because we are about to die if we continue."

"Some things are worth dying for, yes," she said. And I wondered, was she really talking about the rubies? Or something else? That unique woman who did not think she was unique.

I started to reply, but Solo cut me off.

"No stopping now," he said. "Trust me on this, Chewie."

And then he aimed the ship right for the center of the converging threats.

The opening was getting smaller and smaller.

It was the end.

"Pikk Mukmuk!" I cried. "I'm sorry!"

All five burning masses converged on our path.

Voomph!

And suddenly, we were jumping to hyperspace.

"Abort! Abort!" I cried. I knew that the mass cast by all that matter would pull us right back into realspace, where we would die a fiery death as we smashed into the burning wall.

But we did not die. We made the jump!

And suddenly, the *Falcon* was flying smoothly along in that kaleidoscope tunnel of swirling lights.

Mahjo and I looked at each other, blinking in confusion.

I touched my chest. Everything was where it was supposed to be. My head on top. My feet on bottom. All my middle bits in place.

"I am in one piece," I said in amazement. "All of our pieces are where they belong. At least I think so."

Chewbacca started to laugh quietly.

Solo sat back in his chair with the smuggest of all smug grins.

"I don't understand," said Mahjo. "How could we make the jump? Why didn't that wall of stellar matter create mass shadows?"

"Oh, it did, lady," said Solo.

And suddenly, I understood.

"Han Solo, you are a gambler of insane proportion!"

"What did he do?" said Mahjo.

"What did he do? What did he do? He picked the exact point where the gravity of all those burning objects was in perfect balance. We were able to enter hyperspace and stay there, even though it was full of mass shadows, because he found the one spot where they canceled each other out."

I looked at Solo. He was still grinning like the proverbial tooka cat that had eaten the bulabird.

"You had to time that exactly right," I said. "One meter off in any direction and we would not have jumped, and then we would not have had the speed to make it through the gap before it closed. We would have been pulverized into a million little pieces."

"Hey," said Solo, "I got us here, didn't I?"

"Did you?" I asked.

In answer, Solo dropped us out of hyperspace.

And there in front of us hung a radiant red orb—the planet Gwongdeen.

"We made it!" said Mahjo. "We made it to the Undervaults in time!" She started to give Solo a hug, but then she turned and hugged the Wookiee instead.

"Hey, what about me?" said Solo. He looked slightly stung.

I laid a hand on his shoulder.

"It may hurt you to hear this, my friend," I said, "but you are less huggable than a Wookiee."

Solo's mouth began to make funny shapes. But in my years leading the Ohnaka Gang, I had learned that a good leader needs to move things along.

"Well, my friends," I said, clapping my hands, "it looks like profits are on the horizon."

But as we made our approach to that new world, the horizon and everything before it began to look very strange. The uniform red of the planet, glimpsed at a distance, did not seem to change as we got closer and closer. Amazingly, the surface of Gwongdeen was featureless and smooth.

"It's like a giant red pearl," I said. "And somebody has been polishing it."

"A big crimson ball," said Mahjo.

"*Grrrrumppprrr,*" added Chewbacca.

"Or a drop of blood," said Solo.

"I like my metaphor better," I said. "Still, that is not cloud cover we are seeing. That is the planet's surface. But I see no mountains, no hills, no rivers, no cities."

"There aren't any topological features at all," said Solo. "What kind of place have you brought us to now, Mahjo?"

"Just fly to the coordinates I gave you," she said. "You'll see."

"But what is it?" I asked. "Is this a vast ocean? If so, where are the waves, the ripples, the happy sea creatures bobbing up and down in watery joy?"

Mahjo gave me a look.

"I thought you at least would have been to the Undervaults before," she said.

"No," I explained, "this is my first time to Gwongdeen."

"But you knew about it, about the vaults?"

"I knew how hard they were to get into," I said. "That does not mean I had visited them. My dear, you do not get to be a successful pirate by stealing things that are hard to get. No, you steal the easy pickings. As my sweet mother used to say, the easier something is to steal, the more it is asking to be stolen."

Mahjo shook her head, making me wonder again about her past, that woman who could fight, who had been to Gwongdeen but not Dhandu, and who knew some surprising things but not others—and who seemed to have more virtue than her declared profession would suggest. What was she hiding? What was she not telling us? But then we saw other ships on the approach. They were all heading, as we were, to a spot near the equator of that strange world. We fell in a growing line, and then we saw another odd sight.

The ships descended as they reached their destination. But as each vessel was about to touch down, an enormous hole opened in the surface of the world. It was smooth, without any sign of a hinge or a seam. The hole just grew in the red ground, like the gap a bubble might make as it was rising out of a thick liquid, or a tear in a band of rubber that had been stretched too thin.

Then as each ship passed below, the sides of the hole would rush in and close. *Glop! Glop!* It looked too uncomfortably as if the planet were eating them.

"This is not ground, is it?" I observed.

"No," said Mahjo. "It's biological."

"Don't tell me the planet is alive," said Solo. "I hate living planets. I don't want to go to a living planet."

"No, it's nothing like that," said Mahjo. "At least not exactly. You see, Gwongdeen is entirely covered in a biological sea. It's composed of trillions of tiny organisms working together to create a whole. They stretch across the entire world, forming a dense, viscous liquid. It's like the planet is wrapped in a membrane."

More ships disappeared into the sea. *Glop! Glop! Glop!*

"And we're putting down in that?" said Solo. "I just got the ship cleaned."

"You did?" I said. "Because I cannot tell."

Solo harrumphed, but Mahjo spoke before he could respond further.

"You don't need to worry," she said. "The core of the planet is rock. The force fields push the sea back so we can get to the Undervaults beneath. They act as a barrier, both shielding the Undervaults from stellar radiation and making Gwongdeen very hard to visit without permission."

"And we have permission?" asked Solo.

"We do now," said Mahjo, lifting the key. "If we weren't carrying this, we'd never even get inside." She tapped Solo on the shoulder. "Take us down."

"You're the boss, lady."

And then we were descending toward this great expanse of red pudding.

Are you sure you have never been to Gwongdeen? No? That surprises me, it does. Well, let me tell you, it is an experience. As the membrane pulled apart, we could see up close that it was not as uniform as it looked. There were colors and shapes, all the little creatures working together. Like the coral of some oceans—only stickier. And we were descending through it.

But it was not very deep. And then the walls around us changed to the black of a shaft carved into rock. Blinking, winking lights guided us into a vast cavern where we saw an enormous underground spaceport.

Solo and Chewbacca set the *Falcon* down, and we assembled in the starboard airlock, preparing to disembark. Untold riches awaited us, just sitting there for the taking. Or so we thought.

I felt a hand on my shoulder.

"One moment before we go," said Mahjo. "I want

you to know you've all been wonderful. Really. I guess I thought that a band of smugglers and pirates wouldn't be so likable. But you've all been really great. I'll never forget you for your help."

"You sound as if you are saying good-bye?" I said. And although I did not say it aloud, I also thought that once again she did not sound like a person who was experienced in living outside the law. Then I saw her reach a forefinger to tap a slender black band she wore on her opposite wrist.

I had a flash of suspicion. I realized that Mahjo had touched each one of us in the past few minutes. Did she put something on us? I had less than an instant to react. My hand went to my shoulder. My fingers just brushed something small and round, adhered to the fabric of my shirt. What had she stuck on me? I gripped it and pulled, trying to rip away whatever she had placed on me.

"I am," she said. "And I want you to know that I am truly sorry for this."

Mahjo Reeloo's finger depressed the wristband.

I felt a shock like a hundred lightning bolts coursing through my body. I was aware that Han Solo and Chewbacca were also doing the electricity dance beside me.

We dropped to the floor, every muscle in our bodies convulsing.

From my new position on the ground, I could only see the furry back of a Wookiee in front of me, but I heard Mahjo lower the boarding ramp. Then her boots stopped in front of my face.

"I thought if I worked with terrible people," she said, "I wouldn't feel so guilty about double-crossing them. I guess I was wrong."

And then she walked down the ramp and away, leaving us utterly incapacitated and totally betrayed.

CHAPTER 7

ZAPPITY-ZAP-ZAP

I was the first to come around.

Now, you might imagine the Wookiee would have had that position. After all, Chewbacca was bigger than the two of us combined. And he had all that fuzzy stuff to insulate him from the zappity-zap-zap.

But you will recall that I had tried to pull the shocker off of my shoulder just as Mahjo was thumbing it on. So I did not get quite the same dose as the others. And we Weequay are naturally thick-skinned to begin with.

So it was I who shook off the shock before the others. I tore the little round zappy device from my shoulder. It felt good to crunch it under my boot.

Oh, but my head still hurt! And my body—it ached everywhere, like I had been trampled by a herd of skalders. And then trampled again. But I had to get up. I rose to my knees, and that was when I saw that my companions were still out cold. In fact, I think Solo was making little snoring noises. *Rrrronk-shshshsh-rrrronk-shshshshs.*

I don't think you can blame me for having an idea.

I mean, there we were, already at the boarding ramp. And the ramp was lowered. And they were asleep, dead to the world.

It would not be hard to do.

I could just roll them down to the ground—tumble, tumble, tumble. And when they awoke, they would not even know that it was me who had done this thing. Their ship would be gone, bye-bye, and Mahjo Reeloo, the woman who had attacked them, she would be the obvious culprit. No suspicion would fall on me, because they had seen me be zappity-zap-zapped, as well.

Of course, I would not get the Novian rubies. No.

But the *Millennium Falcon* would be mine.

And that, my friend, was a prize worth nearly as much as any Novian ruby. Possibly even more.

As my sweet mother used to say, when the galaxy hands you such an obvious gift, it would be rude not to take it.

So I grabbed Solo first, and I shoved him as gently as time allowed. And I winced only a little bit as I watched him tumbling down the ramp. Over and over he rolled—bumpity, bumpity, bumpity—and then he was off the ship. One more to go, and *my* ship it would be.

Oh, but Chewbacca was harder. The Wookiee weighed a ton. I could not send him tumbling down bumpity,

bumpity. I could not even flop him over. So I ended up grabbing him by the feet and, putting my back into it, dragging him as best I could.

It was sl-o-o-o-o-w going. Let me tell you.

And my poor back hurt so much.

But it would be worth it, if I could just get him off the ship.

And then, before we had even made it halfway, he made a noise.

"*Mmmmwwwww,*" he said. It was the kind of noise you make in the morning when you don't want to get up.

But oh, dear. The zappity-zappity was wearing off. You can imagine the trouble I would be in if Chewbacca came to as I was in the very process of stealing his ship and throwing him off it. You don't have to be an expert on Wookiees to know that the results would not be pretty.

I had to do something.

"Go back to sleepy-sleepy," I said. "You are a sleepy Chewie, a very sleepy Chewie."

"*Mmmmmm . . . rumppppp?*" he said, and his eyelids began to flutter.

Oh, no, what could I do? I was desperate. How to get him to stay asleep? I had a thought. I began to sing softly, a lullaby. Like my sweet mother might have sung to me, if she had not been so busy teaching me to pick pockets.

"Hush, little Wookiee, don't say a word.

"Hondo's going to toss you off this bird."

"Grrrrrrrrrr . . . ooooof?" said Chewbacca.

"And if this bird can fly away,

"This will be Hondo's lucky day."

Chewbacca's eye popped open.

"Uh-oh," I said. I began to pull faster. And sing faster.

"Hush, little Wookiee, don't you cry.

"Hondo just wants to say bye-bye."

A great furry hand reached out and caught the hydraulic lift of the ramp. I tugged his hairy legs as hard as I could, but his grasp was firm.

"And if you—grunt—wake—grunt—before I flee—"

Chewbacca's eyes were fully open. They took in the situation. And then they lit up with angry fire.

"Please, please, little Wookiee . . . don't . . . kill . . . me."

And then I found myself dangling in the air. In mere seconds, Chewbacca had hoisted me aloft and was holding me up like I was nothing but a little rag doll. The grip on my throat tightened.

"You cannot blame a guy for trying," I squeaked.

"Grrr . . ." Chewbacca's growl was low and angry.

"Okay, apparently you can."

"Grrrr, grrrr." Chewbacca growled some more.

This really was the end then. I wondered which of my limbs he would tear off first.

"You know," I said, resigned to my fate, "I used to

be someone. I had a crew. The Ohnaka Gang. I had ships. A tank. I had a beautiful base on Florrum. I had the respect of my people, even when they were trying to betray me. I was Hondo Ohnaka, pirate scourge, and I had the will and the ability to take what I wanted from the galaxy. And what do I have now? I am alone. All alone. Without even a Kowakian monkey-lizard on my shoulder." I sighed deeply. "It is a beautiful ship. I thought . . . I thought . . . with a ship like that. Well, a man could have a second chance. He could find the will to start again. He could go anywhere. Be anything."

Chewbacca glared into my goggles.

"If you don't mind," I said. "I will close my eyes. Because I really don't want to see this coming. The final, hopefully-not-too-painful moments of the once-great Hondo Ohnaka."

I closed my eyes. And I hung in the air listening to the Wookiee's angry breath.

But I did not die.

And then my feet touched the surface of the boarding ramp.

Cautiously, I opened my eyes. Carefully, I felt myself to make sure everything was still in place, my head to my neck, my neck to my body, my body to my limbs. Miraculously, they were all where they were supposed to be.

"I don't understand," I said. "I tried to steal your special ship."

"Grrrragh, rowwwwr, mmmmm, ftttt."

It was the same Wookiee proverb he had quoted earlier, the one about the tree that joins its roots with others underground. He was trying to tell me it was not the ship that was special. I stared at him in surprise, not sure what to say. Fortunately, I didn't get the chance.

"Wh-what's going on?" Behind us, Han Solo was stirring. He sat up and touched his head. "Oh, I don't feel so good." Then he slowly got to his feet. "What happened?"

I looked at the Wookiee. Chewbacca stared back at me. He waited to see what I would say.

"Mahjo Reeloo stunned us," I said. "I woke first, and I was—" I hesitated. Still Chewbacca didn't say anything. "I was trying to rouse you both so that we could go quickly in pursuit of that double-crossing scoundrel of a thief."

It was a lie, of course. Solo studied me for a moment, and I wondered if he could see through me. Then he nodded.

"Well, then what are you two standing around for?" he said. "We owe her one. Let's go pay her back with interest."

With that, Solo went charging down the ramp into the Gwongdeen docks. I turned to Chewbacca, and I gave the Wookiee a grateful look, but he shouldered past me and followed Solo.

You know, I could have turned and run back into the ship right then. I could have slammed the boarding ramp closed and stolen their ship after all, right then and there. But of course, Chewbacca knew that. That was why he went first—and left me alone with the *Falcon*. And that, of course, is why I followed.

Well, I have never been one to dwell on the past. Not with a new, exciting world to explore. There was vengeance to be had. And still the promise of Novian rubies if we could catch up with Mahjo. Despite all that had occurred, the day was looking up.

We made our way to an exit corridor. It was wide, with a ribbed and rounded ceiling—like being in a giant throat. And right down the middle of the corridor was a bright green line. It was maybe half a meter in width, with spots of various colors dotted every few meters. I wondered what their significance was.

Then, as we hurried down the corridor, I saw a being approaching.

It was large, nearly the size of a small speeder. It crawled on the ground with one long, slimy muscle-like foot, and on its back was an enormous shell, as big as a Jawa's hut. From its head, a dozen eyes bobbed on the end of a cluster of tentacles. I approached the creature. It stopped directly in front of us.

"Greetings," I said. "I am Hondo Ohnaka, and these ruffians—excuse me, these distinguished gentlemen—are my associates. I assume you are the Gwongdeen welcoming committee."

The creature did not say anything, just continued to stare at me with its bundle of eyes.

"Yes, yes, of course, we are in a great hurry. So I applaud your decision to dispense with all pleasantries. Can you tell me, did a human woman about so tall pass this way only recently?"

Still there was no response from the creature. I wondered if its vocoder was malfunctioning or something.

"That's our ship," said Solo, pointing behind us with his thumb. "She would have been running from there. Fast. We need to catch her."

Nothing. No response.

"Have we offended you in some way?" I asked. "It is difficult to know all of the local customs. But if you could just direct us to the fastest way to the Undervaults?"

"It's waiting for you to get out of its way," said a human male in a technician's jumpsuit who was approaching us.

"What?" asked Solo.

"The snail," the human said, pointing.

"Do you mean my welcoming committee?"

"Your what? Buddy, have you ever been on Gwongdeen before?"

"No, this is the first time I have had that pleasure."

"Well, then let me introduce you to the local wildlife.

This is a Gwongdeenian sub-subterranean gastropod. And they aren't intelligent. At least, not as far as anybody has been able to determine."

"But it came up to me. It slimed its way right over."

"No, it didn't." The human tapped the ground with his toe, indicating the spotted green line I had noticed earlier. "See these tracks? The snails make them. And then they follow them. That's all they do. All day, all night. You're in its way, and it will stay there until you get out of its way."

"So, these are not for disembarking visitors? They are not direction markings?"

"Not for anything that talks. Just for the snails."

"Great," said Solo as Chewbacca laughed. "We're in a hurry and you're wasting our time talking to a giant slug."

"A snail, not a slug," I told him. "Little details like that may matter." Then I turned back to the technician. "So what are they for? What do you do with them?"

"Nothing," he replied. "Ignore them. That's what everyone else does."

Feeling very foolish, I stepped aside. Immediately, the Gwongdeenian sub-subterranean gastropod began to move forward. I turned as it passed me and watched it make its slow way down the tunnel. I saw people swerving to avoid it, but other than that, the technician was correct. No one paid the creature much attention.

"Live and learn," I said.

Solo stepped close to me and spoke softly into my ear.

"Live and learn," he repeated. "You ever try to steal my ship again, you'll only do one of the two."

And then he smiled and pushed past me.

Well, wasn't that interesting?

We continued on through the strange tunnels. I spotted several more of the sub-subterranean gastropods as we walked. They were everywhere, in fact, the colorful spotted ribbons of their snail tracks crisscrossing the entire underground settlement. Most folks gave them a wide berth, but I did see a group of Rodian children actually riding on the back of one of the creatures. They were laughing and squealing and slapping it on the shell. The gastropod did not seem to mind, as far as I could tell. In fact, it didn't seem to notice them at all.

But soon we came to the entrance of the Undervaults: a great archway, with visitors approaching it.

As we watched, the archway shimmered briefly as each person passed through. But then we saw someone—a little Kitonak—suddenly bump into an invisible barrier. Instantly, security droids converged on the tubby guy, who began protesting that there was a mistake.

"It's some kind of energy shield," said Solo.

"How good of you to state the obvious," I replied. "The key code again?"

"I'd bet on it," he said.

So without the key, our journey was to end there.

Suddenly, Solo yelled.

"There she is!" He took off at a run.

Chewbacca and I looked, and we saw her, too.

That traitor Mahjo Reeloo.

Unfortunately, Solo's sudden movement caught her eye.

She gave us a frightened look, and then she hurried forward, rudely pushing past a group of Togorians.

Solo was almost on her.

And then she passed through the portal.

Solo, unfortunately, did not.

Whump! He slammed into the energy shield barrier.

"Come back here!" he yelled. Then he noticed the Togorians staring at him.

"What's a matter," he said. "You never seen a guy run into an invisible wall before?"

I stopped beside Solo, testing the air gingerly with a finger. It felt as hard and as smooth as a stone to me. I recalled how Mahjo had leapt after Solo and Chewbacca when they fell between the turlossus. Then it had been she who had made me ashamed. And yet the same woman would abandon us now.

"Mahjo," I called. "While I of course applaud your greed, there are riches enough for all of us. Please, come back for Hondo."

She turned then, briefly, and gave me a look—almost of pity.

"I have a lot to make up for already," she said. "Another misdeed won't change anything."

And then she turned and walked away from me.

And there we were, just a few paces apart.

But she might as well have been a whole galaxy away.

"*WWWWWWWGGGGHHHRRRRW,*" yelled Chewbacca. The Togorians scattered at that. So did quite a few other people.

"Well, I don't want to give up, either, big guy," replied Solo. "But we can't follow her without a key code. So unless you have one in that hairy coat of yours, I don't know what we can do."

It was true. Things were looking desperate. But that is when Hondo Ohnaka does his best thinking. We just needed a new perspective.

I looked around. And then I looked up. And then I looked down. And there I saw the answer to our dilemma.

"My friends." I smiled. "Do not worry. I have an idea."

"Will I like this idea?" Solo asked.

"That depends very much on how you feel about getting . . . slimy."

CHAPTER 8

UNDER THE SHELL

"This is the worst plan I've ever heard."

Han Solo was waggling his finger in my face again.

I turned away from him, to where a large Gwongdeenian sub-subterranean gastropod was patiently waiting for us to move out of its way.

"If you will excuse us," I said to the snail, "we will be with you in a moment." Then I turned back to Solo and his waggly finger.

"My friend, do I detect a certain loss of enthusiasm for this endeavor?"

"To lose something," he replied, "means I'd have to have it to begin with."

"Hrrr hrrr hrrr," laughed Chewbacca.

"Yes, yes, very funny," I said. "Now, I do not think you understand the full brilliance of my idea. I will explain it again. It is very simple."

We had walked a little ways from the entrance to the

Undervaults so we would not be lingering and arousing suspicion. The three of us were standing in a nearby corridor away from the main flow of traffic. But like every corridor on Gwongdeen, the ever-present snails were making their steady way, doing whatever it was they did.

I pointed down to the ground, and I tap-tapped my foot right on a snail trail, with its many-colored dots. This one had a nice fuchsia color in the pattern. But that is immaterial. What was important was where it was headed.

"This line," I said, "it runs right through the force barrier. Straight through it. And continues on the other side. Now you don't expect the gastropods to carry key codes, do you?"

"No," grumbled Solo.

"What's that?" I said. "I can't hear you."

"I'm not an idiot," he replied. "Of course the slugs don't have key codes."

"Snails, not slugs," I corrected.

"*Grrrrgrrrrooof,*" said Chewbacca.

"Exactly," I agreed. "But snails or slugs, it would be ridiculous. And yet they come and go, making their snail-y way in and out. Therefore, we can conclude that they are unaffected by the barrier."

"We hope."

"And no one pays them any attention," I continued.

"Everyone just moves out of their way. The locals and regular visitors to Gwongdeen don't even seem to notice them. Am I right?"

Solo's mouth set in a tight frown.

"Am I right?"

Reluctantly, he nodded.

"Very well," I said. "Then here is our solution. Into the snail we all go."

"*Roooarrgh ur roo,*" said Chewbacca.

"It is okay, my furry friend," I said. "The shell is quite large, and the gastropod has no bones. You won't hurt it at all."

"I don't think it was the snail he was worried about," said Solo. And then he added, "I know it's not what I'm worried about."

I placed my hand on the slimy body of the snail and pushed a bit of its blubbery skin aside, exposing a gap under the shell.

"After you," I politely said to Solo.

He bent over. Then he straightened up again, fixing me with another of his hard looks.

"Just so you know," he said, "I have no confidence we can pull this off."

"Well, it's like I always say," I replied with a smile, "no confidence is better than none."

Solo's eyes screwed up at that.

"That doesn't make any—" he began to say, so I

gave him a push, and he reluctantly squeezed his way under the huge shell on the back of the gastropod. He made many *oomph* and *ooof* noises, probably more than were necessary. And then his companion, the mighty Wookiee, followed. And let me tell you, getting a Wookiee to squeeze into a snail—not an easy thing! But finally it was done. Then I, Hondo, slipped under the shell.

It was cramped, yes, for the three of us but not impossibly so. And though there was a wet, mossy smell, it was not unduly unpleasant.

In fact, I was surprised to see it was quite bright. The shell was a very pretty, pearlescent pink on the inside, and the light from outside glowed through the permeable calcium carbonite of it.

We could feel the locomotion as the creature immediately began to move forward once I was out of its way.

"And on we go!" I said. We slid a few centimeters down the corridor.

"Riding to riches!" I added. A few more centimeters passed by in as many minutes.

"Though, of course," I continued, "we are not riding very fast. We are in a snail, after all."

Although the progress was excruciatingly slow, we did eventually return to the main thoroughfare. Through the thin walls of the shell, we could hear the buzz of so many conversations as people made their way into the Undervaults.

Then, rising above the babble of alien voices, I heard the squeal of children.

Suddenly, the gastropod rocked alarmingly. Shadows moved nearby, blocking our light. And the squealing laughter of the children was all around us.

Then we heard a drumming sound and saw the silhouettes of so many tiny hands slapping out discordant beats on the shell.

The Rodian children had returned. They were climbing all over our ride, laughing as they slid over the shell. And pounding, pounding, pounding. They were using us as a giant drum.

Boom-bubba-doom-bubba-doom-doom-doom-dum!

It was most undignified. And it echoed through the shell like we were in the horn of a giant instrument.

And the loud noise was driving the Wookiee crazy.

"EWUUUAUUUGHHHH," he yelled.

The drumming paused for a minute at that. I heard the whisper of surprised children.

"Quiet, my friend," I advised. "Remember, the snails do not make any noise that we have heard. Certainly they do not roar like Wookiees."

"He's right," whispered Han. "Try to keep quiet there, buddy."

But that was no good. The drumming started up again.

Thumpita-thumpita-thump! Boom-bubba-doom-bubba-doom-doom-doom-dum!

"EWUUUAUUUGHHHH," Chewbacca roared again.

Again, the children fell quiet.

I looked at Solo.

"Snails do not shout," I said.

He shrugged.

"Maybe this one does."

Suddenly, a mouth pressed to the shell.

"Helloooo," said a Rodian child, his voice reverberating terribly through our nautilus-shaped chamber. "Hellooooo, Mr. Snail. Anybody in there?"

Were we to be discovered so soon?

Solo gave me a disgusted look. Then he spoke close to the child.

"Yes," he said.

We heard a sharp intake of breath. We heard some excited squeals and more laughter.

"It talks," the child said in awe. "Hey, do you like kids, Mr. Snail?"

"I love them," growled Solo. "I had three for breakfast."

Well, the squealing took on a different tone then. But the drumming stopped. And then we heard cries of alarm and the sound of many little feet scurrying away.

"Well, my friend," I said. "You certainly have a way with children. Perhaps it is a terrible way, but it is a way nonetheless."

"Hey, they're gone, aren't they?" Solo replied.

"*Rrrwwgg,*" agreed Chewbacca, relieved that the drumming had stopped. He put a finger where I think his ear must have been and shook his head to chase away the headache.

Thankfully, the rest of our journey was uneventful. It took us a few more minutes, and then the snail passed through the barrier. We did not feel anything different, but the noise of conversation fell away instantly to be replaced with that hollow silence you always find in a bank or an abandoned starship or maybe a Jedi temple or a library. (Obviously, I have spent more time in the first two of these places than the other two, but I know what they are and I have an excellent imagination.)

"Let me stick a head out and see if it is safe to disembark," I said. Then there was some awkward turnings around, with ungrateful cries of "Get your foot out of my face" and such, and then I was peeking out of the shell. The corridor we found ourselves occupying was thankfully empty, so we slipped out. And it was easier getting out than getting in, though we were left a little slimier for the effort. Solo made a face as he wiped his hand on his jacket. But Chewbacca looked very slick and glistening. Perhaps sub-subterranean gastropod gel agreed with Wookiee hair. I made a note to ask him later. There could be some small profit to be made one day from importing hair product to Kashyyyk.

But that was an undertaking for another time. We were in the famous Undervaults.

Ah, the Undervaults.

They were not like the rounded, ribbed tunnels of the spaceport. No, everything there had been made to appear big and imposing, with hard angles and straight lines, shining stone and gleaming metal. It was all meant to say, *This is a very safe place. If you are even thinking the tiniest little bit about stealing anything from here, well, you had better be thinking of something else, let me tell you that. Because it's not going to work, no.* If that's not exactly what the architect had in mind when they designed the place, well, it's pretty close.

But of course, we were thinking of stealing something—Novian rubies—before it was stolen from us!

Unfortunately, in addition to being big and imposing, the Undervaults were also vast and sprawling. The tunnels went everywhere. They were a repository of gargantuan proportion. They could hide away a galaxy's worth of treasures. And they did! Oh, how I itched to know what was stored in each and every single chamber we passed. Think of the riches! Think of the wonders! Yet all of them were tantalizingly out of reach. We had one goal, one chance at wealth. If we were lucky. If we were fast.

"We should split up and look for Mahjo separately," I said. "We can cover more ground that way. Or should I say, cover more *under*ground."

Solo fixed me with a decidedly untrusting eye.

"You think I'm letting you out of my sight," he said. "You're just as much a double-crosser as Mahjo."

I placed a palm to my heart.

"You wound me terribly, Han Solo," I said.

"Are you going to deny it?"

"What? No. Oh, it is true all right. But in this you can trust me." I looked Chewbacca in the eye. I owed the Wookiee, and he knew it. And I had my pirate's honor.

"Your friend will tell you whether or not you can trust me," I said to Solo. And then I turned and walked away.

When they did not follow, I knew that Chewbacca had vouched for me. So we split up to search for Mahjo.

I do not have the Force, but one does not live long in my profession unless one has a pirate's luck. And that day it meant good fortune, because it was I who found Mahjo Reeloo first.

She was in conversation with a clerk, who was ushering her to a wing of the Undervaults where signs proclaimed that the smaller safety-deposit boxes were kept there.

I walked behind them, trying to look nonchalant and inconspicuous. Yes, I admit, I tend to walk with a bit of swagger, but Hondo can be sneaky-sneaky when it suits him. And right then it suited me.

The clerk led Mahjo to a large room where the floor was covered in circular pits.

Just at the entrance, there was a little table with a round blue tray offering jogan fruit tarts. Of course I helped myself to a few. And let me say that they were very tasty, in case you were wondering.

Just then, a trio of Kyuzo walked past me. One of them turned and gave me a suspicious stare. I returned a wide and friendly smile. The Kyuzo narrowed his eyes. Did I look so shady? I do not know. But I do know from personal experience just how ferocious the Kyuzo can be, and I had no desire to provoke one.

"Jogan tart?" I said, waving a hand at the tray. "They are very fresh."

Rudely, the Kyuzo turned away without even a reply. What has happened to common courtesy, I ask you? But no matter—I had much more important things to worry about just then than the sad decline of manners in the galaxy.

Because suddenly, Mahjo began to turn around. I could not let her see me! But in the open space of the large room, there was nowhere to run, nowhere to hide.

Quickly, I snatched the tray from the table, heedlessly spilling jogan tarts across the floor. I swept the tray up over my head, ducking so my face was covered. Then I fell in line behind the Kyuzo, hoping that the upturned tray would look like the wide-brimmed war helmet these fierce warriors favor.

It must have worked, because Mahjo shrugged off whatever instinct had made her look around and continued with the clerk.

The last Kyuzo in the group noticed me.

"Are you sure you won't have a jogan tart?" I asked him, offering the empty tray. "Oh, look, they are all gone now. Oh, well, it is your loss. You sleep, you weep, as they say."

He grunted and rudely brushed me back. But I was not upset. My deception had worked.

And I saw that Mahjo had accompanied the clerk to a spot that was roughly in the middle of the room. As I followed, I passed the first of the circular pits. I glanced down. The walls of the pit were ringed entirely with black and shiny safety-deposit boxes. They went down as far as I could see, disappearing in the distance below. But there was a turbolift with a short guardrail hovering half a meter or so below the edge of the pit.

The next pit I passed was in use. Way, way, way below, I saw a little blue Narquois opening a box. As I watched, she looked up and glared at me, holding her hand over whatever personal treasure she was placing in there.

I waved to show her I intended no harm. She could keep her secrets; I had bigger burra fish to fry. Then I continued on my way.

The clerk was assisting Mahjo as she stepped alone onto the turbolift of the central pit. It lowered instantly, and I watched as her head dropped below ground level. Her duty done, the clerk immediately turned to walk away.

I needed to act fast.

I broke into a run.

Just then, I saw the long neck of a Kaminoan rise out of an adjacent pit. That caught my eye because you never heard much about the Kaminoans after the Clone Wars. I wondered what this one was up to, and if any of them still practiced their cloning profession.

But I had no time to inquire.

Reaching the edge of the pit and glancing around to make sure no one was paying attention, I leapt.

And I landed with a *whump* next to Mahjo.

I set the turbolift rocking. We both steadied ourselves on the guardrails.

"Hello," I said. "I imagine you are surprised to see me."

She nodded. And then she scowled.

And then she gave me a push.

I was shoved right off the turbolift.

I hung in the air for a moment, arms flailing.

And then I was falling.

CHAPTER 9

A ROBBERY IN REVERSE

This was it.

I was falling to my death.

Just as they say happens, my whole life flashed before my eyes.

And yes, I admit, it was very entertaining viewing. But having been through this a few times that day already, I was wondering if we could just skip to the good bits.

But nonetheless there we were, at the terminus of Hondo Ohnaka's wonderful, exciting career as a dashing buccaneer of the spaceways. The end.

And then . . .

It wasn't the end.

No, I was saved.

At the last possible instant, Mahjo Reeloo reached out and grabbed me. And she pulled me right back onto that turbolift.

I was relieved.

I was surprised.

But mostly I was relieved.

I clapped my hands to my chest.

"I am not dead!" I exclaimed. "This is the second or third time I have not died since I crash-landed on Gwongdeen. What a good day this is turning out to be!"

Mahjo looked at me, surprise on her face.

"You're excited?" she asked.

"Yes," I said. "Why shouldn't I be? I have been saved from certain death. That is something to be excited about indeed. And do not think I am not appreciative to you for catching me. Young woman, you have my sincere thanks."

Well, at those words, the confusion on her face only deepened.

"But—but I was the one who shoved you," she stammered. "It was my fault you were falling to begin with."

"Yes, yes, I know," I replied, waving away her concern. "You shoved me. You caught me. You see, it was the order in which you did it that made the difference. If you had caught me first and shoved me second, it would have been another story, and I would be more upset with you. Well, I would have been dead. But I would have been upset for a moment first. It's these little details that matter most, you know. But you do bring up a good point. Tell me, Mahjo, why *did* you catch me? Although I am of course grateful, it does not seem to have been such a wise move on your part."

She looked over the guardrail, down, down, down into the pit. Then she turned to me with pain in her eyes.

"I couldn't . . . I couldn't do it," she said. "I'm not . . . I'm not . . ."

"Not a killer, no. You have a heart, my friend, and it is not an evil one. You are not a murderer."

"I tried to be."

"Tried and could not do," I said. "You are simply not the scoundrel you led us to believe you were. I did not think you were."

"When did you know?"

"My dear," I said, "it has been obvious to me that you are not very long in this outlaw life. I don't know what reasons have compelled you to try this walk on the wild side, but I don't think the life of a criminal suits you." When she didn't choose to explain, I continued. "It stung, you know."

"I was only doing what I had to," said Mahjo. "I promise you it wasn't personal."

"Personal?" I said. "Do you think that I am talking about my feelings? No. I mean the zappy-zappy thing stung. Have you ever been shocked? It hurts. Now I know why people scream so much when I do it to them. Perhaps I should dial it down in future."

"I thought you were talking about—"

"The double cross? Of course not. My dear, I admire

you for that. It was worthy of Hondo himself. But next time you double-cross me, please find another way and do it without the zappity-zap. And now I will be taking the key, if you please."

Mahjo stiffened as I made a grab for the key, which was clutched in her hand. She moved it away from me as I pretended to snatch for it. And with her attention traveling elsewhere, it was easy to get what I was really after.

But then the turbolift stopped with the slightest of jolts.

Mahjo gave me an uncertain look.

"You still have the key," I said. "And we are here together. So open the safety-deposit box that we have come so far to reach, and let us see these Novian rubies."

She hesitated a moment more, then sighed.

"Very well," she said.

I stood just beside Mahjo.

She selected the right box, inserted the key.

The shiny black drawer slid open.

I peered over the lip of the drawer, expecting a galaxy of riches.

Instead, I saw some old datacards. Some cheap jewelry. A small keepsake holo of a woman, probably someone once dear to Jayyar. Maybe his sweet mama.

But no Novian rubies whatsoever.

I was dumbfounded.

"Where are the jewels?" I said. "Where are my red,

red riches? I don't understand. Why would you double-cross us for a box of useless junk? Where are the Novian rubies?"

"There aren't any," said Mahjo. And I recognized the utter lack of surprise in her voice. Then I knew that she never thought there were. She had lied about the contents of the box. There was never treasure there.

"No rubies," I said bitterly. "This is a terrible disappointment. Ah, you should have let me fall instead of giving such unwelcome news. This is a bad, bad day for Hondo."

Mahjo didn't answer.

Instead I watched as she slipped something from her sleeve into the box.

I only got a quick glance, but the object was shaped like a little egg, only it was made of a sleek black material and had a blinking light on the side.

I wondered what it did and why she had put it there.

Before I could examine it further, she slid the box closed.

"We have to go now," she said.

"I was promised Novian rubies," I replied.

"And there aren't any," she said. "I know. You're angry."

"Let us say that my disappointment currently knows no bounds. Also, I require an explanation. A good one. Then we will see if I am also angry."

"I understand," said Mahjo sadly. "And whatever you

do to me after this doesn't matter. But we have to go now. Do you understand? First we go. Then I'll accept whatever consequences you want."

And she activated the turbolift so it began once again to ascend. And as we rose up, up, up, I thought she looked as though a great weight had been lifted off her shoulders. That was funny—not in a ha-ha way, but in a curious way—because I had caught her, and yet she seemed relieved. I wondered then what the real reason for the rush had been. The rush to get there, and now this rush to leave. Certainly it was not to steal datacards and cheap jewelry. Not for a hologram of someone's mama. And we did not even steal those. There was something else at play, but I was too upset about not being insanely wealthy to work out exactly what.

"I must say, this does not sit well with me," I said. "It is a great waste—sneaking our way into such a protected institution, and to leave with nothing to show for it. If word of this got out, how my reputation would suffer!"

"As a famous pirate?" said Mahjo. "Whatever would the Cloddograns think?"

Her face was down, away from me. But was that just the hint of a sly smile? Yes, she definitely felt as though she had accomplished something. But what, I did not know. But I was glad she was not mopey. I do not like mopey people.

"See?" I said. "Things are looking up." My words were timed so that we had just risen back to the floor level when I made my joke about looking up. We stepped off the turbolift together.

"We need to get farther away, just to be safe," she said, glancing around her. We had the room to ourselves. And then her hand went to the slim controller band on her wrist. Her eyes widened. It wasn't there.

"Where is my controller?" she said, turning accusing eyes toward me.

"Perhaps you lost it," I lied, "in all the excitement when you were zapping us and fleeing the *Falcon*. It could have fallen off then."

Then the accusation in her eyes turned to certainty.

"You did that trick on me!" she exclaimed. "That distracting trick! When you pretended to grab the key code, you weren't after it at all. You took my controller!"

"Do you blame me?" I said. "After what you did to myself and your other companions? Zappy-zappy?"

"Give it to me!" she said. And she made a lunge for me.

Now, I had seen Mahjo fight, and while she might not be a scoundrel at heart, neither was she a pushover. Having fought alongside her, I had no desire to fight against her.

But quick as a flash I was standing by the lip of the next pit. And I dangled her wrist controller band over the yawning space. If my fingers let go, it would fall into the depths.

"I will drop it," I said.

Mahjo went absolutely still.

"You can't," she said.

"Tell me why you want it so badly. Is there another zappy-zappy on my back?" I craned my neck to see, but there was nothing on my body as far as I could tell. She needed it to activate *something*. I remembered the little device she had slipped into Jayyar's box.

"Better yet," I said, "tell me what is so important that you broke into a safety-deposit box only to take nothing out. What did you put in? The little black egg. What is it?"

Mahjo glared, but behind her determination I also saw desperation. Whatever internal war she was waging, she fought it quickly, because then she spoke.

"All right, I'll tell you," she said. "It's a miniaturized defoliator bomb."

"A defoliator bomb?" I repeated. I was amazed. That was leftover Clone Wars technology, and very strong. A defoliator bomb destroys only organic material. Technology is left unharmed, but plant and animal life . . . not so much. It disappears. Poof. Gone!

"And you were carrying this around with you?" I said. "In your pocket? With an activator on your wrist? If you set it off by accident, you would cease to exist! Lady, that is crazy, even for Hondo!"

"It's not like I go around carrying defoliator bombs every day," she said. "I had to have it. I didn't have a choice."

"Where did you even get such technology?" I asked. But then I guessed the answer to my own question. "The Cloddograns. Of course," I said, slapping my free hand to my forehead. "You were buying on the black market."

Mahjo nodded.

"When they saw I came alone, they tried to raise the price on me. I couldn't pay what they wanted and things got ugly. Except that fortunately you happened by."

"Was it fortunate? I think that remains to be seen."

"It was for me, yes."

"Well, you never know what injecting a famous pirate might do to alter the dynamics of a difficult situation. But what do you need a miniaturized defoliator bomb for anyway? And why did you put it in Jayyar Lu-wehs' safety-deposit box?"

"His box didn't matter. It could be any box out of several, as long as it was in the wall nearest the boxes in this pit."

She pointed to the next pit over. The one I had seen the Kaminoan rise out of.

"You see," she continued, "there is something being stored in a box down there. Something very dangerous."

"Ah. You want to destroy this *something* with the defoliator bomb?"

"Yes. I want to destroy it. But there was no way I could break into the right box. Or any box. This place is impregnable."

"And just setting the defoliator bomb off in the pit itself . . . ?"

"Wouldn't work. The door to each safety-deposit box is heavily shielded against just about anything you can shield against. But the insides and backs of the boxes are not."

"So," I said, working it out for myself, "an explosion in the pit would not harm any of the contents of any of the boxes. Because the outside of the box is protected. But inside the box, you are already behind the shielding. An explosion inside one box could destroy any organic contents of another nearby box." I looked from one pit to another. "They are back to back, and their backs are unprotected. You blow it up there, you wipe out the organic matter here."

"Yes."

"Very clever. Very clever. But what is it you want to destroy?"

She took a deep breath.

"That takes some explaining," she said. "You're right I'm not an outlaw. Or at least, not of the sort you mean. This all has to do with a rogue Kaminoan scientist."

"Now that is a coincidence," I said. "I have not heard much of the Kaminoans since the Clone Wars, and here this is the second time I'm encountering them today."

Her expression suddenly grew alarmed.

"The second time?" she said. "When was the first?"

"Why, just a few minutes ago. I saw a Kaminoan rising on a turbolift out of that pit there."

"No!" Mahjo cried. "No, no, no!"

"My friend, what is wrong?" I asked.

"He's come early. He's made the pickup already. We're too late."

"Really," said someone behind us. "Because it looks like *we're* just in time."

We both turned.

There was Han Solo. He had caught up to us.

And he had his blaster out.

CHAPTER 10

GOING SOLO

"Hello, my friend," I called to Han Solo. "I imagine this looks very suspicious."

"You got that right," said Solo, still pointing his blaster at us. He was waving the business end back and forth between Mahjo and me. And his face was all scowly, with his eyebrows doing that crinkling thing.

Well, I could see his anger mounting. The important thing in such a situation was to keep him talking and not blasting.

"Yes, well," I said. "So I can see how one could easily draw the wrong conclusion. Here am I. Here is Mahjo. We have just exited the Undervaults pit side by side. You thought I was chasing her. But now she and I are talking calmly. As if we were in cahoots. Yes, it certainly looks as though we were plotting together against you and the Wookiee."

"I couldn't have said it better myself," said Solo.

"Perhaps I have said it too well," I continued. "And

yet, my friend, would you believe me if I told you that that is not the case?"

"No."

"That is most unfortunate," I said. "And yet, I will say it anyway. That is not the case. You have it all wrong."

"How do you figure that?" said Solo. "Don't expect me to believe you wouldn't pull a double cross for twice your share of the rubies."

"Ha, ha, ha. Yes, of course I would. But while it is certainly true that I would betray you without hesitation for even one single additional Novian ruby (And really, who can blame me? Do you know how much they are worth?), still, I have not done so. Because, you see, and this is the important bit—there are no rubies here."

"Nonsense," said Solo. "You're joking."

"My friend, I do not joke about profits. As much as it pains me to say it, there are no rubies to be had here today."

Solo looked from me to Mahjo.

"What is he talking about, no rubies?" he said to her.

"It's true," Mahjo replied. "I lied about the rubies to get you to bring me here to Gwongdeen."

"I'm having a little trouble believing you," Solo said. "You know, I can have Chewbacca search you both. Ever been searched by a Wookiee? They aren't exactly known for their gentle touch."

"Ha, ha," I laughed again. "I am glad you have still

got your sense of humor. What? Oh, you are not joking." I turned to Mahjo. "My dear, perhaps you had better fill Captain Solo in on everything that you told me."

"*Grrrgarrrr.*"

"Oh, and Chewbacca, as well," I added, seeing the Wookiee had joined us. Then I indicated the entrance to the room, where some more Undervaults patrons were making their way in. "And perhaps you could holster your blaster. It is less conspicuous that way."

Solo's frown shifted from one side of his face to the other, but he put the blaster away. And Mahjo Reeloo told him and Chewie of the real purpose of her trip. As she explained, Solo did not exactly stop frowning, but at least his frown moved around his face in interesting ways.

"Now, my friends," I said when she had finished speaking, "you see that there are no Novian rubies."

"But what's so important that you need to use a defoliator bomb?" asked Solo. "What was in the other box?"

"A thornsuckle plant," she said.

"A what?" Solo replied.

"A thornsuckle."

"I have never heard of it," I said.

"*Grregaaggerrraw,*" agreed Chewbacca.

"That's because it's extinct," she replied. "Or it was supposed to be. It's very deadly, even in small parts.

Look, that Kaminoan Hondo saw. His name is Kolac Pru. He is a rogue scientist who offers his services on the black market. There is nothing Kolac Pru won't do if it means money and a chance to continue practicing his art."

"And how do you know of this?" I asked.

"I . . . I have sources," she said. "But listen. Recently, Kolac Pru was contacted by someone who said they'd found a sample of a thornsuckle plant. Maybe the last one in the galaxy. And they wanted him to replicate it."

"So there would be more?" I asked.

Mahjo nodded.

"They wanted to mass-produce it, to make something that could be injected into a planet's atmosphere. Do you understand? A poison like that could wipe out whole populations."

"What do they want it for?" asked Solo.

"What wouldn't you want it for?" I said. "With such a weapon, you could blackmail an entire planet. You could sell it to the highest bidder. You could even make the Empire do your bidding."

The others were looking at me, their faces a little shocked.

"Do not blame me just because I have a healthy ambition. . . . I am not saying I would do these terrible things, probably, only that I can imagine how someone could."

"Maybe you could imagine with a little less enthusiasm," said Solo. I suppose he had a point.

"Well," I said, "this has all been very interesting, but it is obviously not the concern of a buccaneer such as myself. I am sorry that we do not have a chance to share in profit together, but that being the case, I will take my leave of you."

Solo stared at me a moment, then he turned to Chewbacca.

"Same goes for us, Chewie. This job has already cost us more than we were initially paid."

"No," said Mahjo. "You have to help me."

"Lady, I don't have to do anything," said Solo. "And you have a lot of nerve thinking I'm going to help you now, after you used me to get here."

Mahjo turned her eyes to me.

"Please," she said. "For your pirate's honor."

"I am sorry," I said, "but as I said before, there is only the Empire, those under its boot, and scum like us. If there was some other path, I think you would walk it well. But even if that were so, it is not my walk, and my pirate's honor is not in the mood to help any more today."

I started to leave. And so did Solo.

But Chewbacca did not move.

"Come on, Chewie," said Solo. He turned a shocked face to his hairy friend. "Get a move on, fur ball."

"*Grrraaaaaawrrrrruh,*" said Chewbacca.

"No," said Solo. "We don't stick our necks out when there is nothing for us in it."

"*Rrrrroooooruuuuuu UUUU!*"

"No," said Solo.

"*RRRRRUUUUUUU!*"

Solo's expression was furious. But he turned to Mahjo.

"Chewie wants to know, what's the name of the outfit that is bankrolling Kolac Pru?" he asked.

"It's someone called the Mandragonian Mob," said Mahjo.

"The Mandragonian Mob?" I said in shock, because of all the scoundrels and scum in the galaxy, the Mandragonian Mob was the worst. Worse than the Obsidian Combine. Worse even than the Randolean Ring. The Mandragonian Mob would not just resort to blackmail. They would actually do all the horrible things I had imagined. "That is very bad news."

"It's bad news for the whole galaxy," agreed Solo.

"The whole galaxy," I replied. "Well, it seems we have to do something then. After all, I live in the galaxy."

"*Rurururu,*" agreed Chewbacca.

Solo looked from me to the Wookiee. Then he sighed.

"Great," he said. "This is just great."

"So we are all in," I said. "Very well, Mahjo. You will have the help of three scoundrels. Tell us what to do."

"Well, for starters," she said, stepping onto the turbolift, "let's get my bomb back."

We all jumped on the lift. It wobbled a little bit when Chewbacca stepped on. And then it was down to poor Jayyar's box once again. But when we opened it . . .

"Oh, no," said Mahjo. She held up the little black egg, and I saw that its blinking light had begun to flash very rapidly.

"What now?" grumbled Solo.

"It's the defoliator bomb," she said, lifting it out of the box. "The countdown has started." She looked at me. "You must have bumped the activation button when you lifted the controller band from me."

"Well, turn it off again," I said, and I offered her the controller wristband. But she waved it away.

"I can't," she explained. "Once the countdown has been activated, it's on. This bomb is going off now no matter what."

"How long have we got?" asked Solo.

Mahjo glanced at the display on the tiny bomb.

"Fifteen minutes!"

"Get rid of it!" I yelled.

"I can't. We still need to get this to the thornsuckle before it goes off."

"And be nowhere around when it does," I added. "Don't forget that little detail. Otherwise, bye-bye."

Well, we were off and running after that.

We had to catch Kolac Pru before he left the planet.

Fortunately, we saw him immediately as we ran into the spaceport.

"There he is!" I shouted.

The Kaminoan scientist was moving through the crowd, heading in the direction of the docking bays.

"You have to get him before he reaches his ship," said Mahjo. But even as she directed us, she hung back. I was surprised.

"My friend," I said, "why do you hesitate?"

"He can't see me," she said.

"Why not?" said Solo.

"Because I used to work for him."

Suddenly, many things made sense. Her knowledge of Kolac Pru's business. Her knowledge of the safety-deposit box that Pru used as a drop box for genetic material—she had obviously gone there with him before, at least enough times to have seen Jayyar Lu-wehs using an adjacent box. But mostly what made sense was Mahjo's driving need to make amends for some past wrong.

"But you have to get the thornsuckle," Mahjo said.

"That's not a problem that a good blaster won't solve," said Solo, reaching for his weapon.

"Careful, my friend," I said, resting a hand on his arm. "Do not alert him to our presence too soon, or he may escape us."

Solo nodded, and instinctively he, Chewbacca, and I began spreading out, moving through the crowd. We hoped to converge on Kolac Pru from many sides and stop him that way.

The Kaminoan, with the enormous finlike crests rising high above his long slender neck, was very easy to keep track of. His head bobbed along ahead of us like a balloon on a string. There were not many beings in the spaceport who were taller than he, and one of them was the Wookiee currently creeping along to my left.

Then a swarm of Vulptereen were pushing through the crowd, heading against the general flow. They were everywhere, rudely shoving and squeezing past the other pedestrians. Unfortunately, it had the effect of temporarily separating me from my companions.

So it was that I closed on Kolac Pru first. *Ah, krong it!* I cursed internally, for I still had not replaced my missing blaster. The little details were still tripping me up. No matter—one lone Kaminoan scientist was no match for Hondo Ohnaka.

I reached for Kolac Pru, the end of our arduous adventure finally at hand. The universe would have much to thank me for.

But at the last instant, a figure beside him suddenly moved to block my grasp.

It was a woman. A somewhat *familiar* woman. Human. About so tall. With hair.

I did a double take.

The woman with Kolac Pru—it was Mahjo Reeloo.

But wasn't she behind me, staying back, afraid to be seen? And yet there she was, right in front of me and with Kolac Pru.

"Mahjo?" I said.

The woman's eyes narrowed.

"Who the kriff are you?" she said.

Well, I was stung. And not by a zappity-zappy.

"What do you mean, who am I? I am your companion through hardship and adventure."

The woman shook her head.

"Is Hondo Ohnaka the famous pirate so easy to forget?" I asked.

"Pirate?" said Mahjo, and her eyes narrowed. Then she whipped out a blaster. And she fired it at me.

Well, I was too stunned to move.

And I would be dead, and not telling you this story now, except that suddenly I was knocked from behind.

I tumbled forward, falling to the dirty ground of the spaceport, and the blaster bolt passed over my head. It had missed me by a hair's breadth, which was pretty close considering that my own hair and I had parted company some time before!

I fell on my face, but I was quick to flip over and stand up. You do not live as long as I have by staying down. Then I turned and saw my savior, standing where he had shoved me out of the way.

"Han Solo," I said, "you have saved me!"

"I'm as surprised as you are," he replied.

But then Mahjo Reeloo was lining up another shot, blaster raised to fire again.

And then someone careened into her, knocking her aside.

And that new person, she was also Mahjo Reeloo.

There were two Mahjo Reeloos before me, and they were identical in every respect, including their clothing. The other Mahjo even wore the same slender wrist controller band that worked the zappy-zappy and the defoliator bomb.

"How can this be?" I said. "Two Mahjo Reeloos."

"She's a clone, you idiot," said Solo.

And then I understood.

"Of course, of course, of course," I said. "Of course a Kaminoan scientist would grow his own assistants. Mahjo Reeloo is a clone."

But the new Mahjo Reeloo, she turned her blaster on my Mahjo. I chopped at her wrist with my hand, knocking her blaster off its aim.

It fired into the air.

People around us were screaming. Pedestrians began to run every which way.

"Get to the ship!" the new Mahjo yelled to Kolac Pru.

You know what? From here, let us call her Evil Mahjo to aid in what is going to be a confusing enough situation as it is.

Evil Mahjo and Good Mahjo began to struggle over the blaster.

"Don't let him get away!" Good Mahjo shouted at me.

Well, the two Mahjos looked about evenly matched—no joke—so I ran after Kolac Pru.

To my left, I saw Han Solo converging on the Kaminoan, as well. And to my right, there was Chewbacca, tossing panicking Vulptereens out of his way.

But Kolac Pru was fast—have you seen the long legs on a Kaminoan?

And then he ducked behind a Gwongdeenian sub-subterranean gastropod that was waiting for everyone to get out of its way.

And wouldn't you know it? The Kaminoan had a blaster, too.

Luckily, I threw myself aside at the last minute as the bolts went *bdew-bdew* over my head.

Behind me, I heard the scream of a Vulptereen who was not so lucky.

Behind the cover of the snail, Kolac Pru ran for a cargo bay.

I glanced back to see the two Mahjos still in combat with each other. Then Solo, Chewbacca, and I ran into the bay.

The Kaminoan fired more shots.

There were bundles of cargo boxes everywhere, ready to be loaded for transport.

We ducked behind some, as did he.

"Just give us the thornsuckle!" hollered Solo. "Then you can walk away."

Kolac Pru laughed.

"And double-cross the Mandragonian Mob?" he replied. "I would not walk very far."

Well, it was a standoff, waiting for something in the situation to change.

And then it did.

A further complication!

Because who should come rushing up behind Kolac Pru, blasters blazing, but Trunc Adurmush and his gang of Pakiphantos.

"Oh, look," said Kolac Pru. "My ride is here."

CHAPTER 11

SHOTS AND EXPLOSIONS

"Han Solo? Here?"

Trunc Adurmush was so startled, he blew a long, loud trumpet through his trunk.

"Bawruuuuuuhuuuraaaa!"

Well, any pedestrians who hadn't already run for cover were making themselves scarce then, I can tell you.

"You really get up his nose, don't you, Solo?" I called. Then I saw Trunc Adurmush scowl. After all, he had himself recently been up a nose.

"Oh, I'm so sorry," I added. "I didn't mean to offend. I really blew it there, didn't I? Oh, sorry, I've done it again. I should *nose* better—uh—*know* better. No nose."

"Enough," said Trunc. And he fired his blaster at me. I dove for cover, as did my companions. Solo drew his gun, Chewbacca his bowcaster, and just like that, all the blasters were blasting away again. *Bdew-bdew-bdow.*

Then I saw Kolac Pru slipping away.

"He's making his escape!" I called. But I couldn't go after him. None of us could. We were pinned down.

"I've got an idea!" shouted Solo. "Cover me."

"With what?" I answered.

But Solo was already moving. He ran toward a repulsorcart that held a single cargo container. Giving the cart a shove, he jumped on it.

He stood half-protected by the container, firing his blaster as he sailed closer and closer to the Pakiphantos. He looked very heroic indeed. Or recklessly foolish. Maybe both.

But with everyone focused on Solo, Chewbacca was able to stand and shoot his bowcaster.

Soon Trunc's gang were the ones scattering for cover. What a team that crazy smuggler and the giant Wookiee were!

But we had no time for admiration.

"Hold them here!" I shouted, making a run for it. As I passed, I scooped up a discarded blaster that had been dropped by a Pakiphantos. And I took off after Kolac Pru.

I found him just as he was about to board the Pakiphantos ship. I crept up behind him, my weapon ready, but he spun around at the last minute.

There we were, both of us with weapons pointing at the other at close range.

Neither one of us could survive if either fired.

"Now this is an interesting situation," said Kolac, laughing.

"I admit," I said, "this is a sticky little problem we have here, but if you will just drop the thornsuckle plant, you can be on your way."

"I don't think so. I think you are going to holster your blaster and be on yours."

"If you shoot me, we both die," I said.

"I know," Kolac replied. "But I don't think the infamous Hondo Ohnaka is going to sacrifice his life for a noble cause. After all, there's no profit in it."

"Finally," I said with sincere gratitude, "someone who has heard of me! I could hug you if I weren't trying to shoot you!"

But then I felt something poke me in the back.

"Drop it," someone said.

And there behind me was Evil Mahjo.

I had no choice. I lowered my blaster.

Keeping her gun on me, she strode past to stand alongside Kolac Pru.

"You took your time," he said. "I thought I designed you faster than that."

"The other me proved difficult," Evil Mahjo replied.

"But you dealt with her?" he asked.

"She's dead," said Evil Mahjo.

"Dead?" I said. I was aghast. Although Mahjo had lied to me and tricked me, I genuinely liked her. Or maybe it was *because* she had lied to me and tricked me that I liked her. Either way, I felt a great sadness at her passing.

"Get in the ship," Evil Mahjo said to Kolac Pru. "I'll cover you."

Well, the Kaminoan didn't have to be told twice. He strode quickly onto the ship, taking big steps on long legs.

And I was left facing Mahjo Reeloo's killer, Mahjo Reeloo.

"She was better than you, you know," I said. "It mattered to her that what her creator did harmed so many people. She was looking for a way to atone, to make amends for her part in all of this, and now, I suppose she has done so."

I expected harsh words from Evil Mahjo, but instead her face held sadness.

"She still has a lot to atone for," she said. "And she owes you a great deal, too." Her words surprised me, but still keeping the blaster trained in my direction, she backed onto the ship.

As she held the gun on me, I noticed something about her wrist.

"Wait," I called, starting forward, but the boarding ramp door swung shut. Then I had to jump back as the ship was taking off.

I stood there and watched it go. It was hard to say what I was feeling.

Then behind me, I heard the shouts and blaster fire of Han Solo and Chewbacca versus the gang of Pakiphantos.

Well, they might have some mopping up to do, but they were big boys. One way or another, our adventure was at an end. Kolac Pru was gone. The thornsuckle was with him. As was a Mahjo Reeloo.

I was alone again, and I still needed a way off that planet. A ship. And I knew where there was one.

I made my way hurriedly back to the *Millennium Falcon*. There she was, waiting, just as we had left her.

A quick wiggle-waggle as before, and I was up the boarding ramp and slipping into the cockpit.

I powered up the engines.

But I did not take off.

Something stopped me.

I sat there in the pilot's seat, knowing that with the push of a few buttons, the greatest ship in the galaxy could be mine.

And that was where Han Solo and Chewbacca found me. I guess they dealt with the Pakiphantos faster than I had anticipated. It's these little details that will trip you up, every time.

Solo spun me around in the chair, and I think he would have hit me, but just then a light on the wrist controller flared. Yes, Mahjo's wrist controller. You see, I never gave it back to her.

"What's that?" he asked.

"I think the defoliator bomb has just gone off," I said sadly.

"The bomb?" asked Solo.

"Mahjo was still carrying it," I explained. "But I had the controller."

And then I told him what had transpired. And what I had noticed when Evil Mahjo was backing onto the ship. What I had seen on her wrist—or rather, not seen. The wrist controller was gone.

Do you see? It was Good Mahjo, my Mahjo, who went with Kolac Pru.

"She pretended to be the other Mahjo," I explained, "the new clone, and she left with Kolac."

"But why would she do that?" said Solo.

"It was the only way to be sure," I said. "To be there herself when the bomb destroyed the thornsuckle root."

"She sacrificed herself?" said Solo.

"She has fulfilled the mission she set out to do," I said. "It's over now. She has atoned for whatever evil she thought she helped bring into the world. The thornsuckle plant is no more. And probably Kolac Pru along with it. And . . ."

Beside him, Chewbacca let out a long, mournful moan.

"I know, big guy," said Solo. "I know."

We sat there in silence for a minute, remembering our companion Mahjo Reeloo. Even Solo looked uncharacteristically sad. But not for long. His eyes grew angry again, and he pointed that accusing finger at me.

"You were trying to steal my ship! Again! Weren't you?"

I nodded. No point in denying it.

"I thought I needed a ship. I thought that would give me a purpose in life again. But Mahjo showed me that what I needed was to be part of something that matters. And thank you to Chewbacca, for your Wookiee wisdom. No, I think this ship has a destiny to play in the galaxy, and maybe it is with who it needs to be with for now. But this old pirate has a renewed sense of purpose. Perhaps there are more adventures ahead for me. You know, I am looking for a new crew."

"Oh, no," said Solo. "Not on your life."

"I wasn't asking you," I said. "I was talking to Chewbacca."

"*Grrraggoorarr*," said the Wookiee.

"What do you mean you'll think about it?" snapped Solo.

"*Hu-rruuu, hu-rruuu, hu-ruuu,*" laughed Chewbacca.

"Yuck it up," growled Solo. "And you," he said, pointing at me. "You get off my ship right now. And if I ever see you again, it will be too soon."

"I know you don't mean that," I said, rising from the captain's chair. "But I will be about my way. Just as soon as you give me my portion of the profits from this adventure."

"Your portion of the what?"

"What Mahjo paid you for the initial flight? Certainly you don't think anything that we did could have been accomplished without my help. I want only a modest fee, say thirty percent."

"Get out," said Solo. His face was turning a very interesting shade of red.

"Twenty percent?"

"Out!"

"Well, perhaps we can discuss this later."

"Get off my ship!" Solo yelled.

"Yes, I will see myself out. Good-bye, Captain Solo. Good-bye, Chewbacca, my friend."

And with a farewell from the Wookiee and under the angry gaze of Han Solo, I walked off the *Millennium Falcon*—I wondered if for the last time. But it was not so big a galaxy, and Hondo was bigger. Perhaps our paths would cross again.

And as for Mahjo. Who knows? She had been fortunate indeed to find Hondo. Perhaps luck was with her still. If the Pakiphantos ship was large enough, she might have been able to escape the blast of the defoliator bomb. Perhaps one day I would see her again, too. I thought I would like that.

It had not been a profitable adventure, but it had been a valuable one.

BACK ON BATUU

"**W**ell, there you have it," said Hondo. The old pirate settled back in his chair. He gave Bazine Netal a big smile, looking more than a little pleased with himself.

"There I have what?" she said.

"There you have it," he continued, "the story of the first time I ever saw the *Millennium Falcon*. Such a ship! And what a great time that was! I do often wonder, you know . . ."

Bazine Netal raised an ink-tipped finger to her chin. Despite herself, she had been swept up in Hondo's tale, even if it was delaying her from claiming her prize.

"If Mahjo Reeloo survived the defoliator blast?" she said, finishing his sentence for him.

"What? No," said Hondo. He waved away the suggestion as if it were absurd. "No, no, I wonder—if I had listened to my first impulse and stolen the *Falcon* back then like I originally intended—just what my life would have been like."

"Shorter, probably," said Bazine.

"Ha, ha, ha," laughed Hondo. And then he frowned. "Yes, I believe you are correct. There are only so many times one can upset a Wookiee and live to talk about it. In fact, for most people, there isn't even one time."

"I was thinking more of Han Solo," said Bazine. "He seemed pretty attached to that ship."

"And yet he lost it again, didn't he? And then it lost him. But no, I wouldn't be too concerned about Solo. He was a tooka cat under that gruff exterior. And don't you worry about his harsh words to me there at the end of my story. He did not mean them. I'm sure that he liked me. At least, I'm pretty sure. Well, it may have taken him some time to come around to appreciating my charms."

At that moment, the RX-series droid turned DJ decided to spin a familiar track.

"Ah," said Hondo, "'Mad About Me.' An oldie but a goodie. One of my favorites. I find the sentiment agrees with me very much."

He began to hum along and wag a finger in the air, as if conducting an imaginary orchestra.

Bazine wrinkled her nose. The too-upbeat music got on her nerves. Plus, the swell in the music caused the cantina's other patrons to begin talking louder, so the ambient noise level was going up.

"I think it's overplayed," she said.

"When something works, go with it," said Hondo. "And speaking of something that works, are you sure you wouldn't like a Fuzzy Tauntaun?"

Bazine leaned across the table to stare into the pirate's goggled eyes.

"Do I look like the kind of person who drinks Fuzzy Tauntauns?" she said.

Hondo swallowed.

"Well, to be honest, no," he replied. "You look like you drink the blood of your enemies. But suit yourself. My throat is dry after my wonderful bout of storytelling, so I will get myself a drink even if you don't want one."

He rose, but Bazine grabbed his wrist as he moved to pass her.

"We're not done negotiating," she said.

"No, no, we are not," Hondo agreed. "Far from it. But I have another story to tell you."

Bazine's chin shot up at that.

"Another story? What for?"

Hondo gently eased her fingers from his wrist.

"To further establish the provenance of this fine, fine vessel."

"I thought you just did that," said Bazine.

"Oh, I may have talked you up ten thousand more credits, but after my next tale, you will see that the ship is worth much, much more."

Bazine sighed.

"You aren't going to make this easy, are you?"

"My dear, you can't expect—"

Bazine held up a palm, cutting him off.

"How long is this one going to take?" she said.

Hondo smiled.

"Long enough that I need another drink," he answered. He turned to the room at large.

"Waiter, waiter!" Hondo called out loudly. "Bring me a Gamorrean Grog. And put it on my tab."

"But you never pay your tab," objected the nearest server, a tall blue Togruta.

"I'm glad we are agreed," said Hondo. "Now, fetch me my drink."

He settled back at the table. Remarkably, the Togruta actually did appear a few moments later with a Gamorrean Grog on a tray.

Hondo took a long sip, and then he set the drink on the table and adjusted his hat.

"Now," he said, "here is another tale of the *Millennium Falcon*. And this tale is very special, because this time, I actually got to fly her myself!"

PART TWO

HONDO AND MAZ SAVE THE DAY

CHAPTER 12

MY WORST INTENTIONS GO AWRY. . . .

Frustration.

Do you know the meaning of the word?

The very definition?

For a pirate, it is standing in a parking lot full of ships of every variety from all over the galaxy.

And not being allowed to steal a single, solitary one!

It is like being a kid in a candy shop, without any credits. A kid who doesn't steal, that is. Because a pirate child would just take the candy.

Don't get me wrong. I dearly love Takodana. It is a beautiful place. But it is so hard for me to visit without helping myself to something beyond friendly conversation and a drink while I am there.

Have you ever been?

No, that is a silly question. You must have.

Don't worry. I'm not implying anything. Merely that someone of your particular expertise must get around, and so how could you not be familiar with Takodana and, especially, Maz Kanata's magnificent castle? Or I should say, her once-magnificent castle.

And Maz's castle! With her "no fighting" rules. I cannot tell you what a boon it is to be able to court so many new potential business partners in a place where none of my former business partners are allowed to shoot me! And for some reason I cannot fathom, a surprising number of them want to.

But as I suggested, there is a downside to Maz's rules. So many visitors from across the galaxy, from hardened criminals to bright-eyed explorers, and all arriving in such a variety of strange and wonderful ships. The temptation is too great.

Let me ask you, could it be so bad to steal just one?

Well, one day I did just that. I had gone to Takodana on business, but there she was, parked near the castle, the *Millennium Falcon*.

Sure, it was my friends' ship. But the *Falcon*, she has changed hands before. She would change hands again. Perhaps, I thought, it was time for a new chapter in her book. Oh, she was a little more battered and bruised than when I had last seen her. But she was still a magnificent vessel, and again I felt my heart go patter-pit, patter-pit.

I took a step toward her.

Was I really going to steal her? Maybe I was just going to borrow her for a while. Or maybe I just wanted to sit in that cockpit and dream a little dream. Who can say?

Probably I was going to steal her. After all, I am a pirate, and if people are going to be leaving perfectly good starships lying about, who can blame me if I pick them up?

But before I could figure out what I was going to do, someone spoke behind me.

"Don't even think about it."

Well, I turned around, and who should I see walking away from Maz's castle but my old pal Han Solo and his big fuzzy friend Chewbacca.

"Ah, Solo," I said. "You are looking—" I paused a moment, searching for the right words. "Well, you are looking—" Solo's eyebrow began to rise as I drew my words out. "Well, to be honest, you are looking like a more crumpled and crusty version of the man I met the last time. But I suppose the light that burns brightest burns out first, right?"

He frowned at that, trying to work out if I had insulted him, so I quickly turned my attention to Chewbacca.

"Ah, my Wookiee friend, it has been too long."

"That's still not long enough, if you want my opinion," interrupted Solo. "I warned you before not to mess with my ship."

"Who is messing? And anyway, your ship is a mess already," I said. "But look at the time. I am meeting someone in the castle. So I will take my leave of you. Good day, gentlemen."

"Good riddance," growled Solo. But I knew he was only joking. At least, I think he was joking. I'm pretty sure Solo didn't mean those nasty things he said to me. He was such a kidder, that smuggler.

But as I walked away, I heard a commotion behind me. I turned and saw two very large Dowutins looming up behind my friends. Each of them raised a stun baton. And then zappity-zappity, Han and Chewbacca fell.

Well, Chewbacca had to be zappity-zappitied more than once before he fell. *Ooo, ow, oh.* I winced just watching him. But eventually he went down, too—like a tree in the woods.

That was all very unpleasant and potentially dangerous for yours truly, so I ducked behind another spaceship and watched to see what would happen.

And I saw a little Nosaurian wheel out a repulsorcart, and then the Dowutins unceremoniously dumped my two unfortunate friends onto its flat surface. Then they carted Solo and Chewbacca up the boarding ramp of a little G9 Rigger. And it took off into the blue Takodana sky. Bye-bye.

Well, I felt very bad for Solo and Chewbacca, true.

But then again, fate was clearly handing me the *Falcon.* After all, they couldn't use it themselves—not anymore. It would be a shame to let it go to waste.

So I crept on board, and I made my way to the cockpit. As I sank into the pilot's chair, I just enjoyed the feel of the vessel. The smell of history came off every panel, switch, and button. Also, a little Wookiee stink. Maybe I would install an air freshener later.

I whistled a jaunty little tune while I powered up the ship.

And that's when I felt the barrel of a blaster poking me in the back of my neck.

"Hoooooon-doooooo Ohhhh-naaaa-kaaaa!" The voice was loud in my ear, drawing out each syllable of my name like it was Tepasi taffy.

"There is no need to shout, Maaaaaaz Kaaaa-naaaa-taaaaa," I said, doing the same thing with her name that she'd done with mine.

And then that wiry little pirate was in my face.

"It's good to see you, my friend," I said.

"Don't you 'good to see' me, Hondo," said Maz. "What are you doing here? Get out of the captain's chair."

"What am I doing here? What are *you* doing here? Tell me that."

"Rescuing my boyfriend," she replied.

"Your boyfriend?" Well, that startled me. I knew Han Solo was a ladies' man in his day, but I just didn't see it. But you know, it takes all types to make a galaxy go 'round. Who am I to judge?

"Someone has been stealing ships right here on Takodana," Maz continued.

"Who would do such a thing?" I exclaimed. And I put both hands to my chest to show my shock and outrage—which at that moment, with a blaster pointed at me, was absolutely genuine.

Well, she got right in my face then. And she stared at me, goggle to goggle. Which made me kind of nervous. Her little bitty eyes get quite big.

"Only a fool," she said. And then she added, "So, what are you doing here, Hondo?"

"Me? H-here?" I stammered. "Um, well, obviously, I am rescuing your boyfriend, too."

Maz studied me a moment longer.

"Well, I've got no time to argue with you," she said. Then she sat in the copilot's seat and began to flip switches and punch buttons.

"Shouldn't you be in *Stranger's Fortune* or the *Epoch Swift*?" I asked.

"Faster to take the ship we're in than get mine out of the hangar," she replied. "Take us up."

Well, that little orange lady is not someone I wanted to cross. So we lifted off.

"Where are we going?" I asked.

And then Maz produced a little blippy-blippy device and held it up for me to see. A tiny dot was making its way across a small screen. *Blip, blip, blip.*

"I slipped a tracker into his drink," she said.

"Clever," I said. "But how did you get your ship thieves to drink it? I didn't think you knew who they were."

"Not them," she said. "Solo's drink. That boy will down anything I hand him. And a good thing, too. I asked him and Chewbacca to look into the ship theft for me, but he went at it with his usual subtle touch and got himself kidnapped. But as long as they don't jump out of the system, we can follow. And I don't think they'll be jumping, since they've been running their operation right under my nose."

"Well, it is a tiny nose," I said. Maz frowned at that, so I quickly lifted the *Falcon* into the sky.

"Watch the trees!" shouted Maz.

"Hey, it's trickier than it looks," I replied. "I'm still getting the hang of it." And I clipped off the top of a tree as I spoke.

Then I took the ship into a sharp curve so we passed right over the castle. Perhaps too tight a curve, as I may have grazed one or two towers. "Watch it!" yelled Maz. But on the upside, I got a glimpse of the flag of my old Ohnaka Gang flapping in the breeze coming off Nymeve Lake. Did you know my flag flew on the castle? It did. But no time for nostalgia. We were on our way.

"So what were you doing here, Hondo?" asked Maz as I followed the route of the blippity-blip.

"Oh, just coming to see you, for old time's sake," I said, hoping she would not question me further. "And isn't this fun? Two pirates to the rescue of two smugglers! But tell me more. How exactly did you and your, um, boyfriend get mixed up in this?"

"I've been hearing murmurs of a new gang called the Hackjackers," said Maz. "Word is they've been stealing starships and breaking them down for parts. Now, I don't make it my business what others do in their own territory, but they've had the nerve to steal ships from right outside my castle. So I asked Han and Chewbacca to pose as buyers and sniff them out."

"And they went and got kidnapped," I finished. "Or in Chewbacca's case, Wookiee-napped, I should say."

Maz harrumphed at that.

"This is going to be a long trip if you don't start appreciating my sense of humor," I said. But as it turned out, we didn't have far to go.

Her blippy-blippy thing led us to a small mountain. We hovered above the barren rocky crest. There was nothing below us but rock, vines, and scraggly bushes.

"Oh, well," I said. "It looks like they got away. At least we tried."

"Take her down," said Maz.

"Down? But there is nothing there."

"Down," Maz repeated in a tone that really didn't leave a lot of wiggly room for argument. So down we went. I landed the *Falcon* in a small glen beside the mountain.

Then Maz reached into a storage container, and what did she pull out but Chewbacca's bowcaster.

She held it up and gave me a look that was far too enthusiastic for my tastes. I mean, the weapon was nearly as large as she was!

"You know, Maz," I said, "you should really be careful with that. I've seen it in action, and it packs quite a kick."

"I've seen it in action, too," she said. "But there's nothing like a bowcaster when you want to make a good first impression."

"With a weapon like that, very often no one gets a second impression," I said.

"Let's go," she said.

Now, I was frankly insulted when Maz made me disembark first, as if I really would have left her there and flown away. I would have, but it still hurt to have her thinking so low of me.

And then we were walking through the woods.

"You know," I said, "I am more of a desert person myself. All the little creepy-crawlies in the forests give me the jeebie-heebies. But there is no denying this is a pretty planet you have here."

"You just see that you do your part in this rescue," said Maz, "and I'll let you visit it again."

Oh, ho-ho, that Maz is a kidder. She was kidding, right?

But soon our humor dried up as her blippity-blip led us to a sheer stone wall.

"My dear Maz," I said, "there is nothing here. Your doodaddy device is obviously malfunctioning. I see no choice but to return to the castle, where I would be happy to raise a drink with you in memory of those two brave pilots who were lost this day."

"Don't be such a quitter, Ohnaka," replied the little orange lady. Then she began pushing and prodding at the rock wall.

"Aha!" she said, and she gave a particular stone a twist. Suddenly, a section of the rock wall slid away, revealing a tunnel into the mountain.

Maz turned around and gave me an I-told-you-so look. Then she ducked into the darkness of the tunnel.

I hesitated to follow her. I had a feeling things would get unpleasant where she was going. Whereas, I could still return to the ship and fly away in the *Falcon* if I were quick enough.

"Step it up, Ohnaka!" Maz shouted at me from the darkness.

Well, that settled it. There was no crossing the orange lady—not when she had a bowcaster.

With a last, longing look at the *Millennium Falcon*, I walked out of the Takodana forest and into the mountain.

I hoped I would walk back out again. But that was far from sure.

CHAPTER 13

BASER INSTINCTS IN A SECRET BASE

"**M**az, you know this is crazy," I said as I followed her into the darkness of the tunnel.

"Since when have you let that stop you from doing what you want?" she replied.

"You raise a good point," I said. "But is this what I want?"

"Yes," she said emphatically. "Han and Chewbacca are your friends. Or so you've told me repeatedly."

"Friends, yes," I said. "But my sweet mother always told me, never let friendship get in the way of a good profit. I think she said the same thing about family, too, actually. She did swindle me out of quite a lot of money."

"Is profit all there is to you?" said Maz, snorting.

"Not at all," I replied, stung. "There is also eating and sleeping. Also scheming. And sometimes a little dancing."

"Dancing, huh," said Maz. "Well then, you can shake

a leg. Quit dragging your heels, and let's go free my boyfriend."

Boyfriend. I still didn't see that, but I followed the determined orange lady through the tunnel. Still, I was happy she was taking the lead. And as we got deeper into the darkness, I did drag my heels a little more.

Suddenly, we saw four red dots shining ahead of us.

"What's that?" whispered Maz. "Are those lights? Sensors?"

"You check it out," I said. "I'll wait here and cover you."

Maz made an adjustment to the lenses of her big goggles. Then she peered into the darkness as if she could see better and walked straight forward.

"Maz, I don't think—" I started to say.

Then something furry leapt at us from the shadows.

It had a wide mouth full of sharp teeth.

Its jaws opened wide.

But it did not eat Maz. The wiry little pirate ducked and rolled backward, and the jaws snapped on empty air.

When I had recovered my composure, I saw what it was she had so narrowly avoided—a nexu!

Maz approached to within centimeters of its mouth.

"It's on a chain," she said.

The creature glared at us with each of its four eyes and growled and growled, but Maz was right. It couldn't reach her. It was straining at the end of a large chain hammered into the rock wall. But if Maz had been even a half meter taller, she would have been gobbled up before she could have rolled away.

"That's it," I said. "Time to leave."

Ignoring both me and the snarly beasty, Maz turned in a circle.

"Ah," she said. "The passage doubles back here."

I followed her, being very cautious as I passed the nasty nexu. Sure enough, another passageway led back around, just before the limit of the creature's reach.

"Clever," said Maz. "You can't see the way until you walk past it. But if you don't know about the nexu, you walk too far and get eaten."

"Clearly, whoever lives here doesn't like company," I said. "So maybe we should turn around."

"Hondo Ohnaka, if you turn around now, I'll skin your hide and fly it as a flag over my castle next to the Ohnaka Gang one," she said.

"Well, if you are going to put it that way," I said, "I guess I could stick around a bit more. After all, I am very fond of my hide. I am attached to it, you might say."

Maz did not respond to my joke, but after a little while, the passageway widened into a large cavern, the far wall of which had been worked smooth and set with a large metal door.

Two guards stood there, a human and a Twi'lek. There was no use in hiding—we had been seen—so I gave them my best smile and walked up.

"Hold it right there," the Twi'lek said. "What's today's password?"

"Ah, the password," I said. Then I waggled my fingers in front of their faces.

"You do not need to know the password." I spoke slowly and calmly.

"Yes, yes, we do," said the human guard.

"No, you don't. You do not need to know the password," I said again, and I waggled my fingers some more. "You want to let me enter. You will tell me that I can go about my business."

The Twi'lek blinked at me, then he spoke to his companion.

"I think he's trying to use a Jedi mind trick on us. Are you trying to use a mind trick on us?"

"That depends," I asked. "Is it working?"

"Not so much, no," said the Twi'lek.

"I don't see a lightsaber," said the human guard. "Don't you know you have to be a Jedi to do that trick?"

"Well," I replied, "I have had so many dear friends that were Jedi. I was hoping maybe some of their jumbo mumbo had rubbed off."

"Hey, if you don't have the password," said the Twi'lek, "then you've got bigger problems." And he started to unholster his blaster.

"Time for plan M," I said.

"Don't you mean plan B?" the human replied.

"No," I replied, "I mean plan M. For Maz."

Then I stepped aside, and behind me, the guards saw Maz Kanata holding up Chewbacca's bowcaster.

"I'd be worried if I were you, boys," she said. "I don't actually know how to work this thing."

"Why should that worry us?" said the Twi'lek.

"Because I'm trying to remember if it's possible to set bowcasters to stun, and I don't think that's the case."

After that, the guards saw the wisdom of setting aside their blasters and letting us tie them up. Sometimes a good bowcaster is better than a mind trick.

Then we slipped through the doors.

And there they were.

Han Solo and Chewbacca.

They were suspended in the air, their arms up, like puppets without any strings. And all around the room, I saw many unsavory ruffians. But that was not the center of our attention. There were a host of spacecraft there, and droids were busy tearing them to pieces for their various parts and components.

"This is the chop shop," said Maz. "Right here on Takodana."

"Let's be very quiet," I said to Maz. "They haven't noticed us yet."

"No one operates a chop shop right under my nose," said Maz. And then she yelled *"Arrrrrrrrrr!"* and charged forward with the bowcaster.

Well, that got all the ruffians' attention fast.

Of course, Maz is very famous, and we were on her planet. So quite a few of the ruffians were just standing there gaping at the crazy orange lady bearing down on them.

But then one of them, who had the dark striated skin of a Delphidian, pointed a finger and yelled, "Stop her!"

Well, Maz was not to be stopped.

She hefted Chewbacca's bowcaster, and she fired a plasma energy quarrel.

It missed the Delphidian, but it sure made a big explosion where it hit some cargo crates. They went kaboomy-boom and flew apart in pieces.

Unfortunately, they were not the only things that flew. The little pirate lady was flung backward through the air, and she crashed right into my torso, knocking the wind out of these old lungs.

We both went down in a heap of brown and orange limbs.

Glancing up, I saw that Maz and I were at the center of a ring of very unfriendly faces. Worse, we were also at the center of a ring of blaster barrels. We were captured.

"Well, Maz," I said, "you think you made a good enough first impression?"

CHAPTER 14

HONDO THE HERO

"**D**on't think I'm not happy to see you, Maz," said Han Solo, "but this is about the worst rescue I've been in."

"*Grrraaaarrrrraaaarroooo,*" said Chewbacca, which meant "And that's saying something" in Shyriiwook.

We were all hanging in the air then, our arms over our heads and our legs dangling above the ground. It was actually quite good for my back, but I worried that might not matter very soon.

"You wouldn't need rescuing at all," said Maz, "if you'd played things a little smarter."

"Hey, you asked me to find out what's going on, didn't you?" said Solo. "Now you know."

"This wasn't what I meant. Oh, never mind," said Maz. "Look who I'm talking to."

Well, I thought that was sort of a rough thing to say to your boyfriend, to be sure, but I didn't have long to ponder.

The Delphidian approached us.

"Name's Tjepo Juibop," he said with a nasty grin. "I'm the boss of the Hackjackers. But you're Maz Kanata." He gave the little orange lady an appraising look where she hung in the air. "I must say, it's an honor to have the pirate queen in my hideout."

"What about the honor of the famous pirate Hondo Ohnaka?" I asked. "Do I look like chopped convor liver?"

"Not everything is about you," said Solo. Then he spoke to Tjepo. "By the way, I'm Han Solo. Famous smuggler, hero of the Rebellion."

"*Brrrrgrrrrawwwww,*" said Chewbacca, not one to be left out.

Tjepo shrugged.

"The more the merrier, I suppose," he said. "We weren't ready to move against you yet, Maz, but now we won't have to."

Maz snorted.

"If you thought you were in trouble before," she said, "you've got no idea the trouble you've just bought yourself, mister."

Tjepo laughed.

"Well, I think I've just bought myself a castle," he said. "We'll enjoy taking control of the whole planet now. And there's not a thing you can say about it."

"I might have a word to say myself," I said.

Tjepo looked at me then.

"A word?" he said. "What word?"

"Carbuncle," I replied.

"Carbuncle?" repeated Solo. "What kind of word is that?"

But Tjepo's eyes were going wide in his striated face.

Well, Maz was smarter than Solo. The credit chip dropped for her before the smuggler figured it out.

"Hondo, you old traitor!" she yelled.

"Why? What's he done?" said Solo. "What's carbuncle mean?"

Maz fixed me with an angry look.

"I'm guessing it's today's password," she explained.

"Wait," said Tjepo, and he fixed me with a surprised eye. "You're my buyer?"

"You son of a bantha!" yelled Solo. "I thought you were here to rescue us."

"Rescue, well," I said, "technically, I was more riding along on the rescue. Like an observer. Maz is the real rescuer. So it is her fault it didn't work."

Well, Maz, Chewbacca, and especially Han Solo really had some unkind things to say about yours truly while the Hackjackers lowered me. "I suppose I deserve a small part of that, maybe," I said, "but I didn't know you were going to go and get yourselves kidnapped. I was just on Takodana to see about purchasing some ships and ship components. It was a perfectly legitimate illegitimate business deal before you three had to go and get yourselves involved."

That set off another stream of very nasty things said

about poor Hondo, and I didn't really like hearing them.

"Well, I can't hang around here," I said. Then I realized they were all still hovering above me. "Oh, sorry, I didn't mean hang. I just can't leave things with Tjepo up in the air. Oh, sorry. I mean, it's not like our business negotiations can be suspended—oh, sorry."

Sometimes you have to quit while you are ahead. So I left my friends fuming at me, and I walked off with Tjepo to see what ships and ship parts he had for sale. He really had quite an operation going, and I saw many fine things—flechette torpedoes, sensor jammers, enhanced scopes—so much that a pirate could want. I was like that kid in a candy store again.

Only just then, I heard a commotion high above us. I looked and saw two droids pulling a curtain of hanging vines aside. I realized I was seeing a cavern opening, disguised with vegetation to be invisible from the outside.

And gliding through that newly revealed opening was the *Millennium Falcon*.

"Hey, that's my ship!" called Solo, but nobody paid him any attention.

A little Yuzzum scurried down the boarding ramp.

"We found her parked outside, Boss," the Yuzzum said.

Tjepo walked up to the ship, sizing her up, looking very pleased.

"Quad laser cannons, Arakyd ST2 concussion missile tubes, a BlasTech Ax-108 blaster cannon, duralloy plates, and three deflector shield generators," explained the Yuzzum.

Tjepo whistled.

"That's quite a prize, boys," he called to his gang. "Let's start breaking her down."

"Get away from my ship!" Solo yelled again. But he really couldn't do anything but yell.

I, however, was shocked.

"Breaking her down?" I exclaimed. "Tjepo, my friend, don't you know what this is?"

"Sure," he replied, blinking at me. "It's a Corellian YT-1300 light freighter."

"No," I said. "This is the famous ship, the *Millennium Falcon*."

"It's old," he said. "And it looks like it's barely holding together as it is."

"But the ship . . . it has a history. It fought in the Rebellion. It blew up the Death Star."

"Two Death Stars!" shouted Solo.

Tjepo shrugged.

"It made the Kessel run in less than fourteen parsecs," I added.

"Twelve parsecs!" shouted Solo.

"It's an antique," said Tjepo. "Junk. Trust me, it'll be worth a lot more in pieces."

"Pieces?" yelled Solo. But I nodded. After all, it was a *very* old ship. And I had lots of opportunity to make some good negotiations that day.

Still, I felt sad. And Hondo does not like to feel sad. So I walked away to see what goodies I could find to interest me.

Behind me, I heard the noise of a fusioncutter powering up. Tjepo's men were already starting in on the *Falcon*.

I looked back, and I stopped. I just stood there watching.

I couldn't turn away.

When the fusioncutter sank into the *Falcon*'s hull, I thought I could hear the old bird screaming. I told myself it was just the noise of the fusion beams.

But I knew it was my favorite ship in the whole galaxy dying.

"Oh, well," I said, "nothing lives forever."

Tjepo overheard me say that and laughed. He thought I was talking about the *Falcon*.

But no, I was talking about myself. I excused myself for a moment, to "think over" our negotiations. I pocketed a little fusioncutter, just a small one—good for cutting chains. And when no one was watching, I slipped back into the tunnel.

I picked my way through the dark until I reached the fearsome beast on the chain. I held up the fusioncutter and steeled myself for what I had to do.

Well, you should have seen all their faces when the nexu came bursting out of the tunnel.

It was all snarly and snappy, and its little red eyes were full of hate. Not for Hondo. Hondo had freed it. Hate for poor Tjepo and his Hackjacker gang.

There was shouting and screaming and some crunching and snapping. In all the confusion, no one paid attention to old Hondo when he made his way to his companions.

"Let me get you down, my friends," I said as I turned off the containment field and brought Solo, Chewbacca, and Maz tumbling to the floor.

Maz didn't hesitate.

She snatched up Chewbacca's discarded bowcaster. Then she gave me a dirty look. For a moment, I thought maybe I was on the wrong end of a plasma quarrel.

"Maz," I said, trying to laugh and be friendly, "didn't you learn the first time? What are you doing with that bowcaster?"

"Giving it back to my boyfriend, where it belongs," she said. And she handed it to Chewbacca.

Boyfriend? Chewbacca? Not Solo?

I was dumbfounded.

But as I said, it takes all types to make the galaxy go 'round.

Then Solo was in my face.

"Don't think I'm not going to pay you back for this, you—"

"Yes, yes," I said, interrupting him. "We can negotiate my rescue fee when this is over."

"Rescue fee?" he cried. "That's not what I meant."

But then a blaster bolt flew between us, striking the cavern wall. At least some of Tjepo's gang were not occupied by the nexu and had noticed our escape.

"We'll figure it out later," said Solo. I nodded.

He recovered his blaster, and the fun began.

I say fun, but what I mean is shots firing everywhere—*bdew-bdow*—and the nexu clawing and biting—and the Hackjackers screaming.

We made a break for the *Falcon*, which fortunately was mostly still intact, while Chewbacca laid down some covering fire with his bowcaster.

And we almost made it.

But then there was Tjepo.

He had a big gun, a DLT-19 heavy blaster rifle, and he was pointing it at us.

Well, Solo fired his blaster, just to buy us time, and we dove behind some cargo crates. Tjepo did the same.

"Give up!" Tjepo called.

"You first," I answered. I popped up for a look, but a bolt of plasma energy had me ducking for cover again.

Solo and Chewbacca both tried to get shots off, without success.

"He's too well covered," said Maz. "And we're pinned down."

Solo nodded, but then his eyes went to something

past Tjepo: a rack of stolen weapons and other bits and bobs behind the shipjacker.

"Just keep him talking," Solo said, and he began to move slowly around the corner of the cargo crates.

"Tjepo, my friend," I called, "there is still a way to profit from this day, I am sure."

"You've made a mess of my operations," he called back, "and now you want to talk to me about profits?"

"I always want to talk about profits," I said, raising my head again. "That is what makes me a businessman, and not run-of-the-mill scum like you."

"Hey, I resent that," said Tjepo, and he stood up and fired at me.

But that was the distraction Han Solo needed.

He returned fire. But he was not aiming at Tjepo, who still had very good cover.

No, he was aiming at that rack of weapons and other bits and bobs he had spotted *behind* Tjepo.

Specifically, he was aiming at the shelf of concussion bombs.

And he hit them.

And then everything was going *boom kaboom!*

Well, we raced to the *Falcon*, and I ran to the cockpit and started to sit in the pilot's chair.

Someone grabbed me by the collar and jerked me back.

"My ship, my chair," said Solo, his finger in my face.

"Of course, your ship. I was just warming it up for you. After all, it's your chair."

"And don't you forget it!" he said.

Then we were taking off into the sky, leaving behind . . . well, let's just say that Tjepo Juibop and the Hackjackers were out of business—permanently.

Back at Maz's castle, things were only a little less violent.

"Explain yourself!" yelled Maz. "You were the buyer for the stolen ships!"

"I didn't know they were stolen."

She rolled her tiny eyes at that.

"Okay, I knew they were stolen. But I didn't know they were stolen from here. I am insulted that you think I did. And anyway, you cannot prove it."

"They were going to chop up my ship," said Han.

"Grrrgrrrrgrrr," said Chewbacca, and I don't need to translate that for you to know he was angry.

"Friends," I said, "whatever you think I may have intended to do, I did just save you all at considerable risk to myself. And more important, I saved the *Millennium Falcon.*"

Well, they couldn't argue with that.

Actually, they could, particularly when I brought up the fee for my services. I could tell that I should postpone that conversation for another time.

"I'll just leave now, shall I?" I said. "You can all pay me back later."

And in Chewbacca's case, he did.

BATUU

Hondo stopped speaking and took a big sip of his drink.

"Wonderful, wonderful," he said, leaning back in his chair and propping a foot on the table.

"The drink is that good?" asked Bazine.

"What?" replied the old pirate. "No, the drink is fine, but I was referring to my storytelling abilities. You know, if I did not already have a successful career as a pirate, I bet I could make a go of it writing holodramas. What do you think?"

"You want to know what I think?"

"That is why I asked."

"I think it's time you took me to see the *Falcon*," said Bazine.

Hondo frowned. He had been fishing for praise and gotten none. Then he looked over Bazine's shoulder, scanning the cantina crowd.

Bazine turned to follow his eyes.

She couldn't place where he was looking. But she did notice the little Yarkoran from the card table had reentered the room. The Yarkoran caught her gaze, and he ducked quickly back outside.

Bazine turned back to the Weequay.

"So you've told me why you think the ship is special, and you've told me about how you flew her. Can we negotiate a price now?"

"Almost," said the old pirate. "You must be patient."

"I've been very patient so far," snapped Bazine.

"Then you know how to do it," said Hondo through a big smile. "Relax. I have just one final story."

"Just one?" sighed Bazine.

"Just one. How the ship that I so wanted to steal on so many occasions finally came into my possession. And it was freely given. Freely given, with a catch."

PART THREE

ATTACK OF THE PORGS!

CHAPTER 15

I FINALLY GET THE *FALCON*

The last time I encountered the *Millennium Falcon*, I didn't have to steal it. They actually gave it to me. That's right, they *gave* the *Falcon* to Hondo.

One day, when I least expected it, who should contact me out of the blue but Chewbacca. I was surprised to see his furry little hologram growling at me. I was also sad to learn that my dear friend Han Solo was no longer with him, having gone to that great smugglers' den in the sky. But there was Chewbacca, nonetheless, saying that I, Hondo, was his only hope! Yes, he had come to me. You see, the Wookiee was having problems with his Quadex power core. I understand it had given him trouble in the past, and it was beginning to go out completely. Ah, but the *Falcon* is a very old ship, and as you know, it has been heavily customized. So replacement parts that will actually fit and that will talk to her persnickety computer systems were getting harder and harder for Chewbacca to find.

So after scouting around unsuccessfully for a few weeks, the Wookiee and his new partner—a new Jedi named Rey somebody—turned to old Hondo to see if I could acquire the necessary component. And of course I could. There is nothing Hondo cannot acquire. And I was more than willing to help out my old friend . . . for the right price, of course. Naturally, I wanted a favor in return.

I was thinking of starting a new business venture, Ohnaka Transport Solutions. Doesn't that name roll off the tongue? And although I had amassed many fine ships already, such a fast vessel would be useful in establishing my operation. At least until I got things off the ground, so to speak. Ha-ha. And since the *Falcon* had to be fixed anyway and Chewbacca owed me for my rescue of him and Han Solo, he was more than happy to lend me his vessel for a while. Oh, he acted reluctant. In fact, he drove a hard bargain. I had to throw in some ship parts and tools that he said would help out some of his friends, in addition to the power core, but I am sure that underneath all that grouchy fur, he was actually very pleased.

Still, he said something odd to me in Shyriiwook as he handed over the ship. Now, as I said, I speak the Wookiee language with a bit of an accent. And there are nuances of meaning that sometimes elude me. What it sounded like he was saying was, "Don't mind about all the porgs." But that couldn't be right, could it?

"Watch out for the ports?" I asked. "What's wrong with the ports? Is there a pressure leak?"

"*Prrrrrrgggs,*" growled Chewbacca. "*Krruuuu grrrruuuu prrrrrrgggs.*"

So I had heard him correctly. Porgs. But I had no idea what he was talking about.

"Porgs?" I said. "What's a porg?"

Chewbacca held up his furry hands like he was packing an invisible ball, and then he flapped his fingers. Flappity-flap. And he made a kind of cooing noise—*proo-prooo.*

"*Prrrrrrgggs,*" he said.

"I don't know what you mean, my friend," I said. "Are you making pretend meatballs?"

"*Prrrrrrgggs,*" he said again.

I shrugged. After a moment, Chewbacca did, too. He had given up on trying to make himself understood. So he shook his fuzzy head and walked away.

But I thought maybe I heard him laughing "*Hrrrr hrrrr hrrrr*" as he left me. I stared after him, wondering what was so amusing, and just for a second, I thought I saw something stirring in that satchel hanging from his bandolier. Was it a hint of fluffy movement? Something small peeking out at me? I could not be sure.

Oh, well, I thought. *I guess it doesn't matter whatever a porg is. The ship is mine!*

But as you will see, it mattered very much.

Oh, but it felt good to be alone in the cockpit. And

the *Falcon* didn't fight me so much that time as I powered her up. Perhaps she knew that old Hondo was going to fix her up shipshape and she was excited for the trip.

I lifted off, and I set the course for Batuu. It was a little bit of a stretch to get from where I had met Chewbacca all the way across the Outer Rim to the edge of Wild Space, so I was going to have to make two or three jumps at least. But right then I was feeling peckish. So after plotting the first jump, I went to find the ship's galley, looking for something to eat.

Well, I discovered the refrigerator unit—it was an untidy mess—and I began to rifle through the foodstuffs. I found blue bantha buttermilk biscuits. Blue Bespin breakfast bars. Blue puff cubes. Was everything eatable on this ship blue?

Well, not everything. There were some packets of polystarch dehydration ration packs, but I wouldn't feed that to my worst enemy.

The pickings were pretty slim. But old Hondo knows a thing or two about the culinary arts, so I decided to sauté one of the blue puff cubes in lyseed seasoning and see how it was. Just one for a test. I set it simmering, and I went to check on my flight path.

But as I exited the galley, I got that creepy-crawly feeling that I was being watched—like little buggies up and down the neck. I turned around, but there was no one there.

So I went to the cockpit—everything in order—and I headed back to the galley. I could smell the lyseed simmering. My cooking instincts were correct; this was going to be good.

But when I returned—

The blue puff cube was gone!

Where did it go? I had never cooked with puff cubes before. Did it melt away entirely? I took another out of the refrigeration unit, and I tossed it in the cooker.

Well, it simmered away, but it did not disappear.

And then there it was again, behind me, that feeling of someone looking at my back.

I spun around.

Nothing.

I spun back.

And the blue puff cube was gone again!

"Is someone playing a joke on old Hondo?" I called out. "If so, it is not funny."

And I threw another blue puff cube in to sauté.

I watched it the whole time it cooked. I didn't take my eyes off it.

Not until it was done. Not even then.

I got a plate, but I still watched.

I put it on the plate. I sat down at the table. I cut a piece, and I took a bite.

And oh, it was so good, I closed my eyes for just a moment to savor the flavor.

When I opened them again—

The plate was empty!

Nothing but a lonely lyseed in some oil.

Now, Hondo was starting to feel a little nervous. Was I not alone? Was the *Millennium Falcon* haunted?

"Solo?" I called. "Is that you? You are not trying to spook your old pal Hondo, are you?"

Surely not.

"You're not still mad that I tried to steal your ship? Twice, maybe three times? Come on now, let bygones be bygones."

There was no answer. And I felt very silly. But whatever was happening, I was going to find out.

So very carefully, I put another blue puff cube in the cooker. And then I went to a storage unit and got in, and I left the door open just a tiny crack. And I watched.

And there it was!

A blur of white and brown. A flappity-flap of wings.

A *creature* swooped down from the ceiling and snatched my puff cube away.

"Aha!" I yelled, rushing out. "I've got you!"

And I pounced.

"Aw aw aw," the little creature chirped.

I grabbed for it, but it flapped over my head.

And then there was movement behind me.

Well, I wasn't falling for that again. No.

But then more of the little things came flapping-flapping from under my legs, and to the left and right of me. They were bursting out of the very storage closet I had been hiding in!

I was waving my arms and stumbling in my hurry to get away from the closet. What were these creatures?

Two of them were on the counter. One had one end of the bag of blue puff cubes in its little fuzzy snout, and the other had the bag by the other side.

"Give that here!" I shouted, and I grabbed the bag and snatched it away.

And then, suddenly, everything was quiet again.

And the little things were all staring at me with these big brown eyes.

"So you guys must be the porgs that Chewbacca warned me about," I said. "Well, you're not going to get the better of old Hondo."

They all blinked at once at that. It was kind of creepy and a little bit sad.

Then the first one—the one who had stolen all my puff cubes—suddenly jumped in a little burst of flight, and he grabbed the bag right out of my hand. And away he went racing down the corridor on flappy little feet.

"Come back here with that, you thief!" I cried.

I don't know why I said it. As one who has stolen many things myself, I know that no thief anywhere has ever come back when somebody yelled at them, "Come

back here with that, you thief!" But there I was, yelling those words at a sneaky little bird.

I ran down the corridor into the lounge.

Nothing. No sign of the pesky creature.

"Come out, come out, wherever you are," I said. I pulled my blaster out, but what was I thinking? Because you don't want to fire a blaster inside a spaceship. So I set it down on a nearby container, and I looked around.

He was not in the storage locker. He was not in a basket. Where could he be?

Someone, I saw, had left the holochess table on. All the little holograms were just standing still, waiting for the players to make a move.

No, wait. One of the little holograms was not little. It was quite larger than the others. It was bigger than the Kintan striders. It was bigger than the Mantellian Savrip. And it had fluffy little wings.

I walked over really quiet-like. Nothing moved. Those big brown eyes were staring straight ahead and not blinking. It was almost comical the way he was standing so still. I got down on a knee.

"Aha!" I exclaimed. "You are no hologram!"

With a squawk, the porg leapt into the air, its little flippers scraping across my hat.

I saw the bag of blue puff cubes under the holochess table, so I snatched it up, and then I was running down the corridor.

Well, the porg scurried into the cockpit, and so I did, too.

"This is the end of the line for you, my friend," I said. "And I am using the word *friend* very liberally, because I do not feel very friendly to you, you little pest."

But then the porg turned and sort of meeped, and I looked out the viewport.

The *Falcon* had come out of hyperspace and was waiting for me to plot the next jump.

But there was a ship right in front of me—a pirate ship.

And that's when I heard a boarding clamp locking on to my airlock.

"Meep is right," I said to the porg. "It looks like we are having company."

I started back down the corridor, the porg trailing along behind me—and behind him, a whole bunch of other porgs. I felt like I had a very strange crew indeed.

We got to the airlock just as it popped open with a *chuu-kunk* of shifting metal and escaping gas.

"Now, let me do the talking," I said to the porgs. "Hondo has been all over this galaxy, and many villainous scum are dear friends of mine, so I'm sure whoever it is will understand their mistake in boarding this ship when they see me. Everything will be all righ—"

Well, the words died in my mouth.

Because who in all the galaxy should be facing me but that Pakiphantos scum Trunc Adurmush.

He was, of course, much older than when I'd last seen him. One of his tusks was broken, and it looked like something had taken a bite out of one of his big flappy ears. But I gave him my best smile.

"Trunc," I said, "my old friend. Imagine running into you here. I am so glad to see you up and around, given that the years have obviously not been kind."

Trunc frowned at that, but then he smiled. It was not a nice smile.

"Hondo Ohnaka," he said. "Well, isn't this a great day in the morning? We get our hands on the *Millennium Falcon*, and we get to pay you back for all that trouble you gave me all those years ago." Then Trunc turned to two more Pakiphantos pirates and said, "Grab him, boys."

Well, my hand went to my blaster then. But instead of my blaster, I pulled out a bag of blue puff cubes.

You see, I had set down my blaster in the lounge, and I had holstered the puff cubes by mistake. It's the little details that get you in trouble, I may have said before.

Trunc looked at the bag of blue puff cubes strangely for a minute.

"I've already eaten," he said. "But thanks."

And then I was being unceremoniously bundled away, out of the *Falcon* and into Trunc's much larger ship.

"Help, porgy porgies!" I cried. But craning my neck, I saw no sign of the little feathered critters. They had vanished. And then, as easily as I had gotten the *Falcon*, I lost her.

CHAPTER 16

PUFFY TO THE RESCUE

Well, they bundled me down the hallway pretty fast, and into a holding cell I went.

"You can stew here until we figure out how we're gonna get rid of you," said Trunc.

"Stew would be very nice," I said. "My lunch keeps getting interrupted!"

"You'll live," said Trunc, "though maybe not for very long." And then he laughed at his poor joke, and he left me alone without even a glass of water.

Despondent, I looked at the bag of blue puff cubes. They were pretty crumpled, after my unjust and very rough treatment by the Pakiphantos. What's more, there was a hole in the wrapping where one of those pesky winged fur balls had torn it open with its little sharp teeth. At least half the contents of the package had been spilled.

This is just perfect, I thought. *I am a prisoner. I have lost the Falcon. I am going to be put to death. And I never even got to have lunch.*

I sat there for a while, wondering what I could do, while the Pakiphantos left to search and secure the *Falcon*. And then I had that feeling again, you know, of someone watching me.

I looked up, and there on the other side of my bars, it was that porg. The first one. The lunch thief. A fat little guy with orange plumage around his big eyes. He cocked his head to the side and looked at me—at least I thought it was a he—and then he kind of *proo-proooed* at me.

"It's you, isn't it?" I said. "Come to gloat at me in my misery?"

"*Proo-prooo,*" said the porg.

"Ah," I said, looking where the big brown eyes were pointing. "You just want more puff cubes. You don't care about old Hondo at all, you selfish creature. Well, you can go hungry."

"*Proo prooo proooo,*" said the porg. And that time he looked all sad and mopey.

"Oh, stop it," I said. "I can't stand to see a porg cry. Even if I didn't know what a porg was until this morning."

So I tossed a puff cube through the bars. And he snapped it up so quick, he almost knocked it from the air.

I tossed another, and the little porg leapt to catch it, but in his enthusiasm he banged against the control panel to my cell.

That gave old Hondo an idea.

So I took a third puff cube, and I reached between the bars, and the porg shot into the air and snatched it out of my fingers.

"Not so fast, you greedy little puff ball!" I said. "That is not what I had in mind at all!"

So I was more careful with the next one. I kept my fist closed as I slipped my hand through the bars. And I tossed the puff cube just so.

The porg pounced after it. He bounced off the control panel. And I got a nice electric shock for my efforts.

"Wrong button!" I shouted. But I was happy. I knew the principle of my idea was sound.

So we tried again.

And again.

And again.

I got shocked a few more times. And I worried that maybe the little fellow was going to fill up on blue puff cubes. But I should not have worried. He was a bottomless pit for the stuff.

Finally, it happened.

I tossed a cube directly onto the correct touch button, and he lunged right at it.

And the bars to my cell slid open!

I was free!

Well, that changed my feelings about porgs considerably, I can tell you.

"Thank you, my little friend," I called. And I gave

him another blue puff cube. He puffed up at that and made another *proo-prooo* sound. "I'm going to call you Puffy," I said. "Now let's get out of here, Puffy. Quietly now."

We tiptoed out into the corridor.

And there was a whole flock of porgs—all walking down the hallway with their fat little waddles. *"Proo prooo prooooo,"* they were cooing.

Well, they saw the bag of blue puff cubes and all leapt at me.

So then Hondo was running down the hallway in a cloud of flapping wings and the hungry squawks of plump little birdies.

"Hold it right there," someone said. I pushed flying porgs aside, and I faced one of Trunc's minions. She was raising her blaster.

I tossed a blue puff cube, not at the Pakiphantos but at a control panel. Puffy did his thing, and a blast door slammed into place with the Pakiphantos on the other side.

"Good Puffy!" I said. "Someone has earned another puff cube."

Well, Hondo and his cloud of porgs made it to a weapons locker. And little Puffy, he just jumped at the panel without even being told.

Then I had a blaster.

After a moment's reflection, I turned the setting to stun.

"I wouldn't want you to see anything too upsetting," I said to little Puffy.

And then we were creeping down the corridor toward the *Falcon*.

Or maybe I should say cheeping down the corridor, because the plump little brown-eyed birdies were making a huge amount of noise.

Two of Trunc's gang heard us. But *bdew-bdow* I went. And down they fell.

Then the porgies ran them over, planting little porg feet on big Pakiphantos faces. And we were on our way.

As you might expect, I had to go *bdew-bdow* a few more times, and Puffy, he was crashing into every control panel he saw. If it was on the wall and it lit up, then he would smash into it with tremendous enthusiasm.

And all those other little porgies, they were doing the same thing. They had been watching my Puffy and learning. Soon they were flinging themselves into the control panels with wild abandon—and maybe not such good aim.

Blast doors were rising and lowering. Lights were blinking on and off. Alarms were sounding—*whomp-whomp-whomp!*

Obviously, this attracted some attention.

Two more of Trunc's gang fired at us. And I had to run again.

Unfortunately, I took a wrong turn into the cockpit of their ship.

A Pakiphantos leapt up from the pilot's chair.

I grabbed his trunk and yanked down on it, smashing his head into the dashboard of the ship.

"Sorry, my friend," I said as he passed out. "But if you are going to walk around with such an obvious handle for a nose, someone is going to use it."

But then the porgs washed over me. The cockpit dashboard—it was covered with so many shiny control panels to entice my hungry little friends! They were hopping and jumping all over the place, hurtling into everything that glowed or blinked.

Maneuvering thrusters began to fire up. I heard a hyperspace drive power up and power down. A shout deeper in the ship and a rush of air made me wonder if an airlock had been compromised.

Then someone screamed, "What have you done to my ship?"

I looked, and there was Trunc Adurmush. He was having to steady himself in the doorway of the cockpit, because the ship was rocking so badly.

I was standing in the middle of a swarm of porgs. A stunned Pakiphantos lay at my feet. And all the buttons in the cockpit of the rocking ship were going blinky-blink.

"I imagine this looks bad," I said with a smile.

"What are you smiling for?" asked Trunc.

"Sometimes a smile is all you need to turn a frown upside down," I said.

"Yeah, well, I'll smile once I've peppered you with holes," said Trunc. And then he pointed his blaster at me in a most unfriendly manner.

"Pepper?" I said. "That reminds me. You know, this never would have happened if you hadn't interrupted my lunch."

And then I held up the bag of blue puff cubes, and I tore it open in his face.

And all the little porgies leapt at him, prooing and proooing away.

"Get them off! Get them off!" screamed Trunc.

"Why, Trunc," I said, "whatever is the matter?"

"Get them off!" he yelled again.

And then I realized.

"Are you afraid of birdies?" I asked.

"Yes!" he screamed amid a mass of wings. "Get. Them. Off!"

But I didn't get them off. No, I shoved him aside, and I ran for the *Falcon*.

"Come on, my little friends," I said. And the porgies all raced after me.

Again, we were running down the corridors. *Bdew-bdow*—the blaster bolts were flying behind us.

And we almost made it back to the *Falcon*. The ship

was rocking so badly that I thought the little porgs must have messed with the high-mass electromagnetic gyroscopes. It also sounded like the ion engines and the retro-thrusters were firing in opposition to each other, trying to pull Adurmush's ship apart.

Beside me flapped Puffy. But he was starting to look uncomfortable. In fact, the little guy was burping.

But right before I reached the *Falcon*, I slipped—on a stray puff cube, no less—and down I went.

And then Trunc appeared, standing over me—with his blaster pointed at my face.

"This is as far as you go, Hondo Ohnaka," he said.

"If it is all the same to you," I replied, "I would like to go just a little bit farther."

"Nice try," he said with a chuckle. "But I don't think so. No, it's time to put you out of my misery for good. Any last words?"

"Last words," I said. "Let me think."

If I was going to have last words, I needed to make them count. Then I looked up for inspiration, and I saw, perched all along the bulkheads, my little friends. Only they were all starting to look uncomfortable—gassy and maybe embarrassed.

"Only two," I said.

"Two?" he asked, confused.

"Yes," I said. "Two words." And then I looked at the porgs over Trunc's head, and I shouted my two words.

"Bombs away!"

"Bombs?" said Trunc, confused. "What are you talking about? You don't have any bombs."

"That is correct," I said. "But they do. And I think I've been feeding them entirely too much today."

Trunc turned to look where I indicated. And just at that moment, all those little porgies let loose at once, if you know what I mean.

It was like a fall of snow from the sky, if snow were very stinky and sticky and altogether unpleasant.

Splat, splat, splat, splat, splat!

And Trunc, he was screaming and yelling, bombarded by the remains of all those little porgies' lunch. If he didn't like the porgs before, he really didn't like them then.

He set off running back toward his ship, and the ship was rocking terribly, and he was slipping in the ick.

And Hondo, oh, I was laughing so hard, but not so hard that I couldn't release the docking clamps holding my ship.

And then, when they had finished their business, I raced with my feathered friends back to the *Falcon*.

Straight to the cockpit I went, and into hyperspace we jumped, leaving Trunc's spaceship spinning out of control and, I am sure, in quite a messy state.

"Ha, ha," I laughed with the porgs. "It looks like everything worked out in the *end*."

Okay, that was a bad pun. I admit it. But I was free. The *Falcon* was mine. And I was heading to Batuu.

But I had a small pack of porgs following me everywhere I went.

"What to do with you, my little furry companions," I said to them. "I must say, you are cute when someone gets to know you. Perhaps I could sell you as pets."

Well, Puffy nipped my finger at that—just to let me know his opinion of my plan.

"Oh, you have sharp teeth for a birdy," I said. "But I suppose that quashes the idea. Okay, Hondo promises no selling. I guess you've earned your place on the *Falcon*. Anyway, I think you're going to love it on Batuu."

THE CORELLIAN GAMBIT

"**W**ell, there you have it," said Hondo.

"That's it?" said Bazine. "You're done? That's all there is to say about your history with the *Falcon*?"

"All I feel like talking about today," replied the pirate. "But such fine stories—and most of the bits were true. If I were you, I would be very pleased."

"I'll be pleased when I have the ship," said Bazine.

"And have it you shall. For the right price, of course." The Weequay stood up from the table.

"Come with me," he said. "It is time we draw a line under our negotiations."

Hondo led Bazine out of the cantina and into the streets of Black Spire Outpost.

By then the day was nearly done. The light of the setting sun turned the petrified trees into long shadows that fell across the outpost like the fingers of giant ghosts reaching toward them from the past.

The pirate led the mercenary to the spaceport. There a large facility had been built, partially carved out of the surrounding cliff wall. Towers and cupolas blended with rocklike spires, and a prominent flight tower sat above a large entrance at the base. On the tarmac, there was an enormous collection of cargo crates of various sizes and colors, lumped together alongside scattered tools and other maintenance equipment.

Hondo pointed at the untidy jumble.

"May I present the *Millennium Falcon*," he said.

"What?" said Bazine. "Where?"

"Oh," said Hondo, embarrassed. "I forgot." Then he rummaged in a pocket and pulled out a small controller.

"See?" he said. "I have a blinky-blinky doohickey, too."

Hondo held up the controller and pressed a button.

Suddenly, what looked like cargo crates began to fold up or deflate. Bazine even thought she saw a few of them stand up and walk away on broad metal feet.

When all the decoy crates had folded, shrunk, or ambled away, there it was.

"The *Millennium Falcon*," Hondo said, with a flourish of his hand. "Hide in plain sight, I always say."

Scuffed and scarred, battered and bruised, and yet somehow as splendid as one could imagine. It was almost impossible to believe it was really the *Falcon*.

Bazine was surprised despite herself. After such a

long quest, she expected some sort of trick from the pirate. But no, there was the ship, the loading ramp invitingly lowered.

"After you," said Hondo, and they went inside.

The interior was every bit the mess she predicted it would be. Hondo may have fixed the Quadex power core, but he certainly hadn't done any cleaning.

In fact, several small feathery creatures were nesting in various nooks and crannies.

"The porgs, I presume?" Bazine asked.

"There's Puffy now," said Hondo, indicating a fat little bird and smiling. "Oh, and watch out," he added, pointing at another. "I call that one Snappy."

As if on cue, Hondo's finger strayed too close, and Snappy lunged for it. The Weequay pulled it back hurriedly.

"As you can see," Hondo said with a grimace, "Snappy and I are still working out the finer points of our relationship. Not going to miss *him*, I'll tell you that much."

Then he led Bazine to the cockpit.

Hondo sat in the pilot's chair, then he spun to face her. He stretched his legs out languidly. The pose said, *This is still very much mine until you pay what I want.* Sure enough, he got right to the point.

"And now I name my price," he said. Then he named a very large amount.

Bazine raised a perfectly groomed eyebrow.

"You could buy a small fleet of YT-1300s for that," she said. "It's not like they're new ships."

"But you don't want a new ship, or even another YT-1300," said Hondo. "You want this one. And this one is very special. Special to me personally, as you now know. That raises the price. Also, I don't like dealing in credits. So that raises my price again. Also, it is not technically mine, and I have yet to think of a lie to explain to its owners why I sold it. So that raises the price again. And finally, I threw in a few dozen extra credits as a fee for my excellent storytelling skills."

Bazine rolled her eyes.

"Fine," she said. "It isn't my money anyway." She pulled out a small device and pressed her thumb to a sensor. It beeped softly as figures flashed on a screen. "Done," she said. "You'll find the credits in your account."

Hondo's eyes lit up. "I am almost sorry you didn't barter," he said. "Almost." Then he rose and bowed to her.

"A pleasure doing business with you," he said.

Turning away, Hondo laid a hand on the wall of the *Falcon*.

"Good-bye, old girl," he said. "It has been an experience and then some."

"Oh," he added, and he rested an unwelcome hand on Bazine's shoulder, "and good-bye to you, too, my scary mercenary friend."

Then he walked out of the cockpit and off the ship, leaving the *Falcon* in Bazine's black-fingered hands.

She waited for him to leave, then she slid into the pilot's chair. Taking out the same device she had used earlier, she thumbed a different button.

"I've got it," she said into a transceiver.

After a moment, someone replied. The voice was deliberately distorted to protect its owner's identity.

"Good," the voice said. "Transmitting rendezvous coordinates now."

Bazine checked the coordinates and lifted off. The old Corellian freighter was trickier to fly than she had anticipated, even after hearing Hondo's tales. But she was capable of adapting to tricky situations. And as it turned out, she didn't have far to go.

The rendezvous coordinates took her to Beixander 9, a lonely little moon in a quiet system. She hit the atmosphere and flew across a still ocean to a sleepy spaceport on a hill. She spotted an innocuous light shuttle outside the walls of the settlement and landed beside it.

The contact who met her was a woman—middle-aged, fit. Bazine could tell another fighter when she saw one. The woman looked like she'd been up against it more than a few times.

"I was expecting . . ." began Bazine.

"Your expectations are not my concern," replied the woman. "I will take delivery of the ship now and inform our employer of your success."

"And my payment?" asked Bazine.

The woman scowled as if she were somehow sullying her organization's reputation by dealing with mercenaries and their money matters. But she held up a similar device to Bazine's. The transfer of funds took only an instant. It was a fraction of what Bazine had authorized to be paid to Hondo for the ship. But it was still a large amount for a job where she hadn't been required to kill anyone or place herself in too much physical jeopardy. Good. It was done.

Bazine looked at the shuttle.

"I suppose a lift would be too much to ask?"

"It would," said the woman. "We are not a taxi service for mercenary scum."

"Beixander isn't exactly a bustling port," argued Bazine.

"That's obviously why we chose it for this delivery," said the woman. "You have been well compensated for your efforts. You'll be able to hire a lift off-moon . . . eventually. But you had better hurry. The settlement has a curfew in place. It will shut its gates for the night soon, and you wouldn't want to be alone out here when any of Beixander's nocturnal fauna come out to play."

Bazine stared at the woman. She didn't like her. But the job was done. There was no sense hanging around.

The mercenary turned away—the *Falcon* wasn't her problem anymore—and hurried to the small outpost, hoping she could at least find decent lodging before everything shut down for the evening.

The woman watched her go. Then, completely ignoring her own shuttle, she boarded the *Falcon*. Reaching the cockpit, she took off.

Hondo was still waiting in the docking bay of his transport enterprise when the *Millennium Falcon* landed again.

He didn't act at all surprised to see the woman striding down the loading ramp.

When she approached him, he flashed her a big smile.

"Welcome to Black Spire Outpost," he said, his smile widening, "Mahjo Reeloo."

"Hondo Ohnaka," said Mahjo. "It's good to see you in person."

"I am sure that it is," said the pirate. "But did you have any trouble?"

"It was tricky, but thanks to the device you planted on her shoulder, I was able to hack into her communicates and learn the location of their rendezvous."

"And the real contact who was supposed to meet Bazine?"

"I hit her with what you called my zappity-zap," said Mahjo.

"Oh, ho-ho-ho," said Hondo, "I don't envy her at all. I know how that feels."

Mahjo looked at him earnestly then.

"It's no Novian ruby," she said, "but I hope you think this favor finally makes us even for the trick I played on you all those years ago."

Hondo waved a hand dismissively.

"It was for a good cause," he said. "As was this. For old friends, some of them gone, and, well, I know this ship has a history helping out the good guys. I am sure it has not reached the end of its days assisting the rebels."

"Resistance," corrected Mahjo.

"Rebels. Resistance. Bah, they are all the same to me. Underdogs. Do you know I am a hero of the Liberation of Lothal?"

"I do," said Mahjo. "You've told me many times."

"So I have. So I have. And what of you?" said Hondo. "Do you feel as though you have finally made up for your past mistakes?"

"I don't know," said Mahjo. "But I've spent my life trying. No reason to stop now."

"I'm glad," said Hondo. "The good guys need scoundrels, too, if they are to make it."

Mahjo smiled to be called a scoundrel. Coming from Hondo, it was an honor.

"But what happens if Bazine figures out she was tricked?" she asked.

"She has no reason to come back here," said the pirate. "You tricked her, not me. I sold her the ship fair and square, and she cannot prove otherwise. What she did with the *Falcon* afterward is her concern. But if I were Bazine Netal, I would not be quite so eager to tell my employers that I had the ship but I gave it away—to the Resistance, no less—and took a large price for it, too. No, I wouldn't want to be in her shoes then."

As he talked, Hondo led Mahjo from the docking bay back into the streets of Black Spire Outpost.

"But come," he said. "I am feeling generous. I will buy you a drink. In fact, I think I finally have enough to pay off my tab at Oga Garra's cantina."

"My goodness," said Mahjo. "That must be some tab."

Inside the cantina, Hondo was approached by the small Yarkoran from the sabacc game.

"You did well, my friend," said Hondo. "Thank you for contacting Mahjo Reeloo while I stalled Bazine Netal with my excellent storytelling abilities. Tell Og I want to buy you a drink. She can put it on my tab."

"I thought you said you were going to pay off your tab," said Mahjo, smiling.

"I said I *could* pay my tab," explained Hondo. "I didn't say I was going to. But grab yourself a drink, too, both of you, and give me a moment. I need to speak to an old friend."

When his companions stepped away to the bar, Hondo pulled out a small transceiver.

"*Grrrarrragagha,*" said the person on the other end.

"The ship is safe, my friend, and we are even," Hondo told Chewbacca.

"*Ooooorrrrrrrhuuffff,*" said the Wookiee.

"Have no fear," replied Hondo. "I will bring her back to you when I am done with her. Or not."

"*Arrrrgoooorrroof?*" said Chewbacca.

But Hondo Ohnaka, pirate, scoundrel, smuggler, and storyteller, disconnected the call.

"Now," he said, "with all that unpleasantness out of the way, I just need to find a good crew, and I am in business."

Hondo walked over to a bulletin board in the cantina. Tearing off someone else's flyer, he printed something neatly on the reverse side. Then he affixed the new advertisement to the bulletin board and stood back to admire his handiwork. The sign he had created read:

Flight Crews Wanted
No training necessary.
Fair pay, great experience. Discretion a must.
Inquire at Ohnaka Transport Solutions in the Spaceport.

"Good, good," said the old pirate with a smile. "I wonder who will apply for the job first." Then he turned and spoke to the room at large.

"Today was a good day for profit. Let's see what tonight brings! I'm feeling lucky. Anyone for a game of sabacc?"

Lou Anders is the author of *Frostborn*, *Nightborn*, and *Skyborn*, the Thrones & Bones series of fantasy adventure novels. Each of the books, in addition to being an exciting story full of heroes and monsters, contains rules for an original board game that Anders created. He is also the recipient of a Hugo Award for editing and a Chesley Award for art direction, and he was named a Thurber House Children's Writer-in-Residence in 2016. Anders lives in Birmingham, Alabama, with his wife, two children, and a golden-doodle named Hadley. He first visited a galaxy far, far away when he was ten years old and has wanted to fly the *Millennium Falcon* ever since. He knows that the Force will be with him always and hopes it will be with you, too. You can visit him online at louanders.com and on Facebook, Tumblr, and Twitter @Louanders.

Annie Wu is an illustrator currently living in Chicago. She is best known for her work in comics, including DC's Black Canary and Marvel's Hawkeye. Her previous work for *Star Wars* includes *Lando's Luck* by Justina Ireland and the Join the Resistance series by Ben Acker & Ben Blacker.